Can this party be saved?

 After the long walk home, I rang the doorbell, still in high spirits from our successful package hunt. Mom opened the door, and as soon as I saw her face I knew something was wrong. Behind her, I could see kids running back and forth and toys all over the place. It didn't look like a party. It looked like a disaster area.

Ask your bookseller for these other PARTY LINE titles:

#2 JULIE'S BOY PROBLEM

#3 BECKY'S SUPER SECRET (June, 1990)

#4 ROSIE'S POPULARITY PLAN (July, 1990)

Special party tips in every book!

ALLIE'S WILD SURPRISE

by Carrie Austen

SPLASH™

A BERKLEY / SPLASH BOOK

ALLIE'S WILD SURPRISE

One

You know that TV show *Memorable Moments*, where people get to tell their most memorable moment and the audience votes on whether it's worth a bar of soap, a toaster oven, or a trip to Hawaii? Well, if someone said to me, "Allison Gray, what was your most memorable moment?" I'd have to say, without a doubt, it was the day The Party Line was born.

I'll never forget it because that was the day my best friend, Becky Bartlett, got her greatest idea ever—to start our own business throwing parties for people.

Actually, it happened by accident; it's just that Becky knew how to take advantage of the situation. See, there are four partners—me, Becky, Julie Berger, and Rosie Torres—but none of us had actually planned on starting a party business. That's how things are sometimes. If you're in the right place at the right time, amazing things can happen.

The Friday before, I had to pick up my little

brother Mouse from nursery school. Everyone else in my family calls him Jonathan, which is his real name. I call him Mouse because the first sound I ever heard him make was a little squeak, just like a mouse. His nursery school is only a couple of streets over from my school, Canfield Middle School, where Becky and I are in seventh grade.

Outside Mouse's school, I read the notices on the bulletin board while I waited for the kids to come out. Some were put up by Taylor College students looking for part-time jobs or rooms to rent. Some were about special events on the Taylor campus, which is in the middle of town. That's when I saw a poster announcing a Vermilion concert at the college. I couldn't believe it. Vermilion was actually coming to Canfield!

Mouse appeared, and before he knew what hit him I was pulling him down the street.

"Come on!" I shouted.

"Where are we going?" he asked, running beside me.

"To Becky's," I said. I could hardly wait to tell her about the concert. Becky is the only person in the world who really understands what Vermilion means to me. I mean, everyone (except maybe my parents) loves Vermilion. She's the best, really fresh.

She has a great voice, she's a fabulous dancer, and she wears the most fantastic clothes that she layers and mixes in terrific combinations, like denim and lace, or glittery, shimmery scarves that blow all around whenever she moves. She has long curly red hair and beautiful violet-blue eyes. All my friends have Vermilion's albums, but I feel a special connection with her because I read that she used to stutter when she was little, and learned to sing and perform in spite of it!

I don't stutter very badly, but sometimes I get a little tongue-tied when I'm rattled or if I have to talk in front of a big group of people. I couldn't imagine being Vermilion, performing in front of huge crowds. I get stage fright. I can't even try out for glee club. I have a pretty good voice and I watch Vermilion's videos to learn all the dance steps. But I couldn't do it in front of anyone, except maybe Becky.

I let go of Mouse's hand and he skipped ahead of me and up the wooden stairs to the Moondance Café. Becky lives there. Well, upstairs, actually. Her parents—Becky's mom and Russell, her stepfather—own the whole house, but the first floor is their restaurant.

I pushed open the doors.

"Anybody here?" I called. The main dining room was empty, but its blue calico tablecloths and matching curtains looked cheerful and ready for company. A big grandfather clock against the back wall chimed once as the hands moved to three-thirty.

The sound of squeaky wheels shattered the silence. David, Becky's brother, came out of one of the small dining rooms, pushing a cart full of dishes toward the kitchen. He saw us and waved. I wondered if I should ask him where Becky was, but he wasn't looking at us anymore and I felt weird. I mean, David is fifteen, so he's not *that* much older than me. But sometimes he seems a *lot* older.

Suddenly the kitchen door burst open as Becky backed out, carrying a tray of sugar bowls. Becky is the only person I know who can speedwalk backward.

"Watch out!" cried David, stopping just in time to avoid a collision. It was a good thing, too, or the floor would have been knee-deep in broken glass.

"David, this is not the Indianapolis Speedway, you know," snapped Becky.

David whistled through his teeth. "You're a walking disaster area," he grumbled, heading toward the kitchen. "But at least there are witnesses!"

Becky turned to see me and Mouse standing there. Somehow I managed to wait until the swinging doors had closed behind David before I blurted out my great news.

"Becky! Vermilion's doing a concert at the college!"

"Taylor College?" Becky said in amazement. "That's *incredible*! When is it?"

"In two weeks," I said. "I read about it on the

bulletin board when I picked Mouse up. Becky, we just have to go—"

Becky held up a hand and shushed me. "Wait a second, Allie. Let's get Mouse settled first. Then we can talk, okay?" Becky turned toward Mouse and helped him off with his jacket. Then she began showing him how to fill the sugar bowls with little white and pink packets.

Becky is always so thoughtful. In my excitement I'd practically forgotten Mouse, and he was *my* brother. He seemed thrilled to have such an important job and was happily concentrating on it when Becky flung herself into a chair in front of me.

"Okay. Tell me everything about this concert we're going to."

"You'll go with me, really?" It wouldn't have been hard to convince Becky to go with me, but I was glad she'd said it first.

In the first place, how could I miss it?" she said. "And in the second place, you'd make me go with you anyway, right?" I nodded. "So how much are the tickets?"

I looked at my shoes. This was the part I hadn't been looking forward to. "Eighteen dollars."

"Each?"

"Uh-huh. For good seats. I mean, it doesn't make any sense to sit somewhere where we can't see her."

"Allie! How can we go? Where will we get almost forty dollars?"

"I don't know. Try to think of something." Becky had to say yes. I needed her moral support. She had been with me through most of what my dad called my "Vermilion phase." It wasn't a phase, though. Becky understood how I felt. She knew how much I adored Vermilion, how I practiced singing and dancing to her videos. This is not so easy if you're shy like I am and you have a houseful of brothers and sisters who never give you any privacy. So I practice a lot over at Becky's. There's an old full-length mirror in her attic and it really helps me get all the moves right. Best of all, the attic is our own special place, and no one ever comes up when we're there.

"Now, if I could have a real job here at the café, like David. . . ." Becky started.

I had heard this before. Becky had always wanted to work at the Moondance, but she was so incredibly klutzy that her parents only gave her safe things to do, away from glassware and sharp objects and especially away from the food. It really bugged her.

"It looks like you *are* working here, Becky. What are you doing?" I pointed to the table in front of us, which was covered with napkins folded into fancy pleated half-circles. This had to be Becky's work. I could just tell.

"This?" She picked up a napkin, shook it out, and folded it back up again in about three seconds. "This is monkey work. And unpaid labor, I might add. I get to fold all the napkins. I get to fill the sugar bowls with sugar packets. Big deal." She brightened. "This is my Japanese fan specialty. Like it?" I nodded and Becky grimaced again. "My parents always expect me to mess up anything more complicated."

I giggled. "Maybe they're afraid history will repeat itself, like the time you put raisins in the potato salad."

"Well, I thought that was a good idea! If raisins are so good in carrot salad, how come it's so awful to put them in potato salad?"

"The green food dye in the cream pitchers?"

"It was St. Patrick's Day! Nobody has any holiday spirit around here." But Becky was starting to grin in spite of herself.

"Then there was the time you knocked over the dessert cart. I never saw your mom as mad as she was that day, scraping blueberry pie off the wall during the dinner rush."

"That was hardly my fault!" shouted Becky. "I had to jump out of the way when that waiter came charging through carrying a dish of flaming duck. How was I supposed to know they'd moved the dessert cart? If it had been where it was supposed to be. . . ."

"Oh, Becky." I sighed. "You never mean to do any of the things you do. You . . . you're just . . . unlucky, I guess," I finished lamely.

Becky scowled. I looked at the napkins. She might be dangerous around breakable objects and her creative ideas might backfire sometimes, but Becky could always come up with good ideas for decorating, or something to do, or just about anything. Right then I was hoping she'd come up with an idea that would get us to the concert.

"Will you just think about some way we can earn—" I tried to add eighteen and eighteen in my head—"thirty-eight dollars?"

"Sure," she answered. "And by the way, it's thirty-*six* dollars. The concert's in two weeks, huh? We'll have to think of something fast."

I felt so much better. I could almost hear the wheels turning in Becky's head.

"We get our allowances tomorrow," I said, to sort of get her in the money spirit.

"And keep them for about five minutes," she said.

Becky was not exaggerating. There was always something she just had to have. Her parents refused to give her an advance on her allowance anymore; otherwise she'd spend money she didn't even have yet. I'm not a whole lot better with my allowance, either.

"We could walk dogs," she said. "Or exterminate mice. Casey Wyatt makes a fortune getting rid of mice and spiders and things from people's basements." Casey is in our class, but we avoid him whenever possible. His idea of something funny is to put a live worm in your desk. Or worse—in your lunch!

"Ee-yew!" I said, mimicking my sister Caroline's

favorite expression. "That definitely sounds like Casey."

"Babysitting would be all right if we could get the really good jobs. Which we can't." The older kids in the neighborhood get the best jobs because they can stay out late.

"Besides, I do enough babysitting," I added. I spend a lot of time babysitting for my little brothers and sister—Mike, who's ten, Caroline, who's eight, and Mouse, who had just turned four. Suzanne is older than me—she's fourteen—but she hates baby-sitting, so I do her share of it while she takes over my dishwashing duty, which is what I hate the most. Usually it works out fine.

"That reminds me. I have to help get ready for Mouse's birthday party tomorrow. My mom hired a clown to entertain at the party, but I think I'm go-ing to decorate before he gets there. Come on, Mouse, time to go."

"Wait! Before you go. . . ." Becky picked up a nap-kin. "I invented a way to fold napkins so they look like rabbits. Maybe you can use this for the party." She shook out the napkin and smoothed it out.

"Watch that glass!"

"Oops!" Becky caught the glass just as it was about to fall.

As Becky's fingers flew over the napkin, I looked around. I really loved the Moondance Café, or any-place in Becky's house, actually. There's always a crowd at my house. At Becky's there's only her brother and her parents, so there's lots of space. Besides Becky's room, which is pretty big and even has a fireplace, there's the porch in nice weather, the restaurant, and, of course, the enormous attic Becky's mom lets us use.

"There. How's that?" Becky held up the napkin with two points coming out of the top.

"It's . . . uh . . . fine," I said, shifting my book bag to a more comfortable position.

"But?" Becky stared at me.

"Well, it doesn't really look like a rabbit."

"What does it look like?" Becky stood with her arms folded.

"A napkin with a knot in it."

Becky's mouth twitched. "Tell me the truth," she said. "Is this idea better or worse than raisins in potato salad?"

"Um, better," I said. "But. . . ."

"But nothing! There's hope yet!" Becky giggled. "Come on, I'll walk you to the door."

"Are we meeting Rosie and Julie tomorrow?" I asked. Rosie and Julie and Becky and I are all best friends. The thing that's really neat is that we all get along so well even though we're all pretty different from each other.

"Of course we're meeting them," Becky said. "At the Wishbone at eleven-thirty."

The Wishbone is this crazy store in the Pine Tree

Mall that has really wild stuff, like clear plastic telephones with neon lights inside them and pencil cases shaped like bananas. My mother can't stand the Wishbone. She says it gives her a headache just to look in the window. We have a lot of fun browsing there, though, and at birthdays we try to buy one another's presents there. One year I got Rosie a pair of earrings that looked like tropical fish and were made of feathers. That's the sort of thing you can find only at the Wishbone. Rosie still wears them, too.

"Great," I told Becky. "Come over around eleven and we'll walk to the mall together, okay?"

"Okay."

"And don't forget to think up some brilliant money-making ideas. We've *got* to go to that concert!"

"I'll work on it," she promised.

Two

I got up early the next morning, even though it was a Saturday. Mom had asked me to help with the party decorations. I didn't mind—I loved doing that kind of thing. But I needed an early start to get everything done before I left for the mall.

I put on my stonewashed black jeans, my red sweatshirt, and a pair of red high-tops. I counted my money one more time. With today's allowance I'd have $6.35, but I still had to buy Mouse's present. Whatever I had left over afterward I'd put in my concert fund.

I wolfed down breakfast in record time and got to work in the dining room. I climbed on a chair and tacked up streamers. When I was finished, yellow twists of crepe paper crisscrossed each other above the table. I had decided to make dinosaur shapes for decorations and to use as place cards. I spread out Mouse's picture encyclopedia of dinosaurs, colored construction paper, markers, and scissors. With a

Vermilion tape on to keep me in the mood, I copied shapes of different dinosaurs onto the construction paper and cut them out. Mouse came in to see what I was doing.

"This one is Charlie," he said, walking a purple stegosaurus across the table.

I blew up a big bunch of balloons. Mouse tried to help, but as hard as he puffed he just couldn't managed to get any air in them.

I hung my dinosaur shapes and a few balloons from the streamers overhead and tied balloons to each chair. I cleared the dining room table and put a dinosaur place card and a bag of candy at each place.

Mouse snuck a gummy dinosaur when he thought I wasn't looking.

It was almost all ready when Dad returned with the birthday cake.

"Allison," he said, putting the cake box on the counter that separates the kitchen from the dining room, "do you think you could play a different tape? You must've played this one ten times today. Even I can recite the lyrics now. 'You are my on-leeeeee one,' " he sang in a loud, out-of-tune voice. My dad likes to tease.

The doorbell rang. It was Becky, exactly on time for once.

"Wow!" she said. "This looks terrific!"

"Didn't she do a great job?" added Mom.

"You really think so?" I liked what I had done, but it made me feel great that other people liked it, too. "Thanks," I said, grateful for the compliments.

"Hey, happy birthday, Jonathan," said Becky. "I have a present for you. I made it myself." She held out a brightly wrapped package.

When Mouse opened it, his eyes got round. He pulled out a Tyrannosaurus rex made out of a blown-out egg, cardboard, and green paint.

"Oh boy!" he said, holding it up for everyone to see. "Thanks, Becky."

"Becky, you're so clever!" said my mom. As we went out the door she reminded us, "Don't forget to come back for birthday cake later."

Three

Outside in the fresh air I forgot about dinosaurs and birthday parties and began thinking about the concert. I wondered if I'd be able to get close enough to say something to Vermilion. Now *that* would be incredible.

When we got to the Wishbone Julie and Rosie were already there, looking at exotic jewelry.

"Hi!" said Becky.

Julie looked up. Today her smooth blond hair was pulled back from her face with a blue headband that matched her eyes. Her wide smile, gleaming silver from her braces, shone out when she saw us. "Hi!"

"Aren't these great?" said Rosie, holding up a pair of earrings that had all kinds of tiny fruit hanging from thin chains. There was a necklace to match. Rosie's dark wavy hair bounced as she turned from side to side, trying to see how the earrings would look alongside her heart-shaped face.

I wanted to look around, but I just knew I wouldn't

be able to relax until I'd bought Mouse's present. I've always been that way. My friends are used to it, and even tease me about it sometimes because I always have homework and school reports done way ahead of time.

"The earrings are nice, Rosie," I said, "but . . . um, c-could. . . ."

"Allie has to get Mouse a birthday present," Becky cut in, smiling.

"Well, let's get the toy store out of the way," said Julie. Rosie put the earrings back with a wistful sigh.

We walked side by side through the mall and turned in at The Toy Chest. I found the perfect gift: a big plastic model of Tyrannosaurus rex with a movable head and tail. It was only $3.99, plus tax. I had $2.20 left.

We went into Winter's, a big department store. Julie bought a pin that said I ♥ Cats. She and her sisters have a very spoiled Siamese cat named Dizzy. I wished I could buy something for myself, but it was more important to see Vermilion. And to do that I'd have to save every cent.

"Look at this!" I cried, lifting a purple hat from a rack. It had a long curled feather sticking out of the brim. I tried it on and looked in the mirror. "What do you think?"

In the mirror I saw Becky poke her head over my shoulder. She pulled the feather under her nose like a mustache, and I cracked up. Then she tried on a big red floppy hat backwards, and Julie started to giggle. By the time Rosie tried on a black top hat with silver sequins, we were all laughing, even though she actually looked good in it. Rosie seems to look good in anything.

When we got to the makeup counter, with all the testers, Rosie decided to experiment on Becky. Rosie always does this sort of thing, and we never mind. She's good at it.

First Rosie pushed Becky's hair back from her face. Then she stood back and looked at her from all angles, just like an artist. Then she chose brushes and dabbed at colors, brushing and smoothing things with cotton balls from the salesperson, who was fascinated by the whole thing. Rosie lined Becky's lips with one color lipstick and filled them in with another.

The salesperson nodded in approval. "You ought to get a job here," she said to Rosie.

While all this was going on, Julie and I sampled the lipsticks and even took a few squirts from the perfume testers at the next counter. By the time we left Winter's, Becky looked like a cover girl and the rest of us smelled like a flower garden.

"Liz Barrow's brother works here," Julie said as we passed the On Track sporting goods store. Liz was in our class at school. "He works at the cash register," Julie went on. "I heard he's really cute!"

"Let's go in," said Rosie, interested.

"Yeah, I need some new tennis clothes," Julie answered, giggling. Julie had never played tennis in her life.

Becky and I looked at each other and rolled our eyes. Julie and Rosie are both a little boy-crazy. Becky and I couldn't care less. I mean, we weren't about to make a special trip into On Track just to see a boy.

"I'll wait out here," I said, sliding down to sit in front of the store, putting my package down while I took my jacket off. Shopping is hard work.

Becky flopped down beside me, and we watched people go by, looking inside now and then to see what Julie and Rosie were up to. They had gone through the entire rack of tennis clothes. Now they were going through the men's soccer shirts.

"Do you see what they're doing?" asked Becky. "It's so obvious!"

"I know. I'd die of embarrassment if it were me."

"Here they come. Finally!"

We stood up as Rosie and Julie came out.

"He really *is* cute!" said Rosie. "He has the most gorgeous blue eyes."

"And he's tall, and he has a nice smile," said Julie, grinning from ear to ear. You could tell she was dazzled by Liz Barrow's brother.

"You two!" Becky said in mock exasperation.

"*You* two!" said Rosie and Julie at the same time. We all laughed.

After On Track, we stopped in the record store. Rosie, Julie, and Becky looked through records while I headed to the section where tapes were on display. I looked wistfully at the two Vermilion tapes I still didn't have.

"You buying them?" Becky was suddenly at my elbow.

"No," I said, putting them back in the rack.

"Oh, Allie," said Becky. "I wish I could resist temptation the way you do." She clutched a Jesse Barrett record. "Here goes my allowance!"

"I'm not just being good, Becky," I pointed out. "Even if I weren't saving for the concert, I couldn't buy it anyway. Mouse's birthday present pretty much wiped me out." My allowance was a little smaller than Becky's anyway—another drawback of a big family.

We went up front and Becky paid for the album. Then we just rambled all the way through the mall, looking in windows. Becky and I were in front and Julie and Rosie were right behind us, laughing about something. Boys, probably. Suddenly I stopped. My package—with Mouse's present—was gone!

Four

"When did you see it last?"

"Did you leave it in the store?"

"Do you remember putting it down?"

"Are you sure it wasn't stolen?"

The questions came so fast I didn't even know who was asking them. All I knew was that I had a knot in the middle of my stomach. What if I didn't find the package?

"I . . . I d-don't know," I said. I couldn't remember. We had been in so many places.

"Look," said Julie, "there's only one way to do this. We have to do a systematic search. We'll retrace our steps, and go back exactly the way we came."

Julie had studied how to be a detective last year, when she thought she wanted to be a private eye. (Now she was more interested in baseball, and wanted to be the first woman player in the major leagues.) What she said made sense, and we agreed to try it.

We went back to every store, starting with the last one, the record store. I felt shy, but I went up to the cashier.

"Excuse me," I began. "I, um, lost a p-package, and I, um, w-wondered if someone here f-found it." My friends all made sympathetic faces. They know that I stammer especially badly when I'm upset.

The woman checked under the counter.

"Sorry, I'm afraid there's nothing here," she said. "Come back later. Maybe someone will turn it in."

"Thanks," I said.

We hiked back toward Winter's. Julie wanted to stop and go into On Track again.

Sure, I thought, *to get another look at Liz's brother.* I tried not to show my impatience. "I didn't go in there, Julie," I told her, and kept walking.

We checked the perfume counter as well as the jewelry, handbag, and hat sections at Winter's. "Try the lost and found," said the last salesperson, pointing to the back of the store. We marched through the aisles toward the office. A bored-looking girl asked me what I wanted.

"I, uh, l-lost something and I wondered if s-someone turned it in," I said.

"It's a package," added Becky, with a sense of urgency. "A Toy Chest bag."

"It had a dinosaur inside," Julie added.

Rosie giggled. "Sorry," she whispered. "It just sounded funny."

The girl seemed annoyed with us for disturbing her. She left her chair and went into a back room. She poked her head out to ask, "When did you lose it?" and again moments later to ask, "Where did you lose it?" as though she couldn't handle the answers to both questions at the same time.

The lost and found didn't have it. We ran out of there, trying to hold our comments until we were clear of the store.

"Wow!" said Julie. "She didn't like us because we asked her to do her *job!*"

"She was bordering on brain-dead!" said Becky. "Didn't she know that if you knew *when* you lost it and *where* you lost it, it probably wouldn't *be* lost?"

We went all the way back to The Toy Chest. The salesperson remembered me, but said I hadn't left my package behind. I knew she was right. I remember having it with me when we walked along from store to store. I just couldn't put my finger on when it was first gone.

While we were in the toy store, I saw small rubbery miniature dinosaurs on the counter for $1.99 each. I was so upset about the lost dinosaur, and so worried I wouldn't find it, that with the last of my money I bought a tiny brontosaurus for Mouse, just in case. With a sick feeling, I looked at my change.

Thirteen cents. I put the coins in my pocket and tried not to think about it.

"I still think we should try On Track," said Julie.

"We might as well," said Rosie.

"But I didn't go in there. Only you and Julie did, remember? I waited outside with Becky."

"That's true," said Julie. "But we should cover every possibility, no matter how slim the chances are. Come on, Rosie." Julie and Rosie went inside for the second time while Becky and I watched through the window. I was too nervous to go in. I didn't see how my package could be there, but we'd looked everywhere else.

I watched Rosie and Julie go up to the boy at the cash register. When he smiled and reached down behind the counter, I couldn't believe it! He came up with my package!

When they came out, Julie pushed the package at me and ran away before I could even thank her.

"What happened?" I asked.

"She's embarrassed," said Rosie. "Look, she's turning red."

We all raced after Julie, and collapsed in a heap on a bench in front of a bakery.

Becky giggled. "Julie, I didn't think anything ever embarrassed you! I never saw you blush before. Look!" We all watched, fascinated, as the red in Julie's face crept up along the part in her hair, like a thermometer.

"What did he say to you?"

Julie finally caught her breath and spoke. "He said someone found the package outside the store and brought it in. But he winked when he said it."

"So?"

"So now he thinks we planned the whole thing just to meet him!"

I felt bad that Julie was upset, but I was really relieved to have gotten Mouse's present back. "Oh, Julie, I must've left it there when we sat outside waiting for you. I'm sorry! But thanks a lot for getting it back for me."

"Oh, smell that?" said Rosie, twitching her nose. "Why did we have to sit in front of a bakery? It's driving me crazy."

It did smell good—sweet and warm, like a freshly-baked cookie. I suddenly felt very hungry.

"Let's get something to eat," said Julie, fully recovered now. "I'm starving."

"You're always starving," Becky said. "But you're right, it's definitely lunchtime. I could eat a horse."

"Me, too," I said.

We headed off toward the food court, the part of the mall where you can get all kinds of food: french fries, pizza, hot pretzels, tacos, you name it.

There was a table for four being wiped clean by an attendant. We pounced on it as soon as he was done.

"Let's take turns going up for food," suggested

Becky. "That way someone will always be here to keep an eye on our stuff."

Everyone agreed, and Becky and I went first. I was aiming for the taco stand, but when I reached into my pocket and felt my change, it jogged my memory.

"I'm skipping lunch," I said.

"What?" said Becky. "I thought you were hungry."

"I changed my mind," I said.

Becky looked at me. "Oh, come on, Allie. I'll lend you some money." Becky is one of the most generous people I know.

"That's okay," I said. It would be hard enough to get the money for a concert ticket without owing Becky money in the bargain. I went back to the table and sat down.

Julie and Rosie went for their food and came back with Becky. Becky put a plain paper plate and empty paper cup in front of me.

"What's this?" I asked.

"Your lunch," said Becky, breaking off a piece of her hamburger and dumping half her french fries on my plate.

Julie cut a triangle off her pizza, and Rosie broke off part of her jumbo eggroll. "It's a little messy, but good," Rosie said.

"This is more food than you guys have!" I yelled.

But I felt good, and not just because my stomach had been grumbling.

Julie poured some of her soda into my cup. Becky and Rosie did the same. Of course, they were all different flavors, so I had something that tasted cola-fruity. It was delicious.

"Hey, guys," I said. "I'm sorry about before. Thanks for finding my package. I never would have gotten it back without you."

"That's okay," said Julie, grinning. "I'm glad the detective work paid off."

"The four of us make a great team, don't we?" Rosie added.

"Save room," I reminded everybody. "My mom told us to come back and have some birthday cake."

"Hurray!" said Julie.

"Pig out!" said Becky.

Five

After the long walk home, I rang the doorbell, still in high spirits from our successful package hunt. Mom opened the door, and as soon as I saw her face I knew something was wrong. Behind her, I could see kids running back and forth and toys all over the place. It didn't look like a party. It looked like a disaster area.

"Oh," she said in a small voice. "Hi. Come on in."

"Mom, what happened? Where's the clown?" I asked.

Mom ushered us in as though she were guiding us through a war zone. Dad was in one corner of the living room trying to calm down little Danny Ogden and Philip Gurney, who were fighting over Mouse's dump truck. He looked up and smiled wanly when he saw us. Another little boy sat nearby, sniffling and sucking his thumb.

"The clown called just after you left. He's got the

flu and couldn't make it." I'd never seen Mom look so frazzled. "We've really had our hands full trying to keep an army of four-year-olds entertained. I persuaded Jonathan to share his toys, but he's not too happy about it."

In the dining room, one little girl sat at the table, eating the candy out of the other children's goody bags. Uneaten cake sat on paper plates. Julie peered at one of the plates.

"Why do these plates say Happy New Year?" she asked.

My mother shrugged. "The clown was supposed to bring all the supplies: cups, plates, napkins, you know," she explained. "This was all I had left in the house."

"How much longer is the party supposed to last?" asked Becky.

"The parents are coming to pick up their kids at three-thirty."

I looked at my watch. "An hour and a half to go," I announced grimly.

"I have an idea," said Becky. "I'll be right back." She flew out the door before we could ask her what her idea was.

Rosie went into the living room and sat down. She reached into her bag for a marker and a small sketch pad and drew a big circle on one of the pages. (Rosie's a true artist. She never goes anywhere without her pad and pens.)

"Where shall I put the eyes?" she asked a little girl who happened to be nearby. Two other kids became curious and walked over, and all three of them pointed to a spot on the paper. Rosie drew in great big googly eyes with long lashes.

"And what about the mouth?" Again, the children pointed. The two boys fighting over the dump truck soon stopped playing tug of war with it and wandered over to see what was going on.

Julie grabbed the balloons from the dining room chairs and brought them in to Rosie.

"Maybe you can draw faces on these," she suggested.

"Great!" said Rosie. "Who wants a balloon face?"

The shouts of "Me! Me! Me!" were unanimous.

For each kid Rosie painted on any face he or she wanted—normal faces, happy faces, even horrible monster faces. Mom and I were standing there, completely absorbed, when Becky came back in, letting the door slam behind her.

"Follow me," Becky said. She grabbed my arm and practically dragged me down the hall. We ducked into the den, and Becky shut the door.

"Here. Put this on." She handed me something made of yellow and red cloth.

"What is it?"

"A clown suit. I found it in the attic a couple of days ago. I also brought my old magic set. Remember it?" She showed me her magic wand, a painted black stick with a silver tip, and I suddenly remembered one Christmas when Becky got that magic kit and learned one trick after another, using me as her audience.

"You put on the clown suit and be my assistant, okay? It's a little too short for me, but it should fit you just fine."

"Okay," I said, slipping the costume on over my jeans and sweatshirt.

When Mom saw me in the baggy clown suit, she laughed. "You girls are amazing!" she cried. "Julie and Rosie have the kids wrapped around their little fingers with those balloon faces, and now this!"

Actually, most of us had done some babysitting, so we knew preschoolers needed plenty of lively entertainment.

Mom ran upstairs and came back with her makeup kit. "Let's get you in the right mood," she said, still laughing. I was glad to see her looking a little more like her calm, cheerful old self again. She did something around my eyes with eye shadow and an eyebrow pencil, then put lipstick and rouge on me and dabbed a spot of red on the tip of my nose. Now I knew how Becky had felt in Winter's.

"I'll do your face, too, Becky," she said. Becky plunked down on the chair and Mom leaned over with her eyeshadow brush. "Well, it looks like someone got here first," she said, noticing what was left of Rosie's makeup artistry. "I hate to paint a silly clown face over something so lovely."

"Oh, you know how much Rosie loves fooling around at the cosmetic counters," said Becky. "Go ahead and give me a funny face. Saving the party is more important than saving my makeover."

Mom carefully painted a sprinkling of red freckles across Becky's cheeks, and finished by giving her a round red nose to match mine.

"There! Instant clown!"

The clown suit and all the makeup made us feel clowny. We silly-walked into the living room. The children were sitting in a circle around Rosie.

Rosie pointed to us. "Look who's here!"

The children were delighted to see us and crowded around, their balloon faces bobbing in the air above their heads. Julie got them all seated in a semicircle, and we were ready to begin. Between the grinning children and the balloons, we had a pretty big audience.

Becky's magic show was a great success. (I wasn't bad myself as her assistant.) Danny and Philip were now the best of friends, trying to figure out how Becky found coins in their ears. Jason Plummer watched in fascination as Becky put a marble into a little plastic box, closed it, then opened it again to show that the marble had disappeared.

I checked the time. We still had forty minutes left.

"Mom, you already gave the kids birthday cake, right?" I asked, when the magic show was over.

"Not exactly," she said. "They didn't eat it."

Dad took over. "Well, I checked the spelling on the cake when I picked it up, and it looked like the right color icing, but. . . ."

"It's not chocolate, and the kids hate it. I think it's mocha," Mom finished.

What else could go wrong?

"Is there any ice cream in the freezer?" I asked, trying to think of some way around the cake problem.

"Just bits of this and that. Everything in there has been opened."

I went into the kitchen and pulled out all the half-used cartons of ice cream from the freezer. Then I took out eight small bowls. I dropped a gummy dinosaur into one before spooning out the ice cream. I mixed a little of every flavor in each bowl and then stuck a candle in the middle and a chocolate cookie on the side.

We called the kids into the dining room for their "prehistoric ice cream." Julie marched them to the table in a dinosaur parade, with Mouse at the head as Tyrannosaurus rex, king of the dinosaurs, because it was his birthday. Recalling the names from the encyclopedia this morning, I called off names for the other kids.

"Stegosaurus. Allosaurus. Diplodocus. Brontosaurus. Triceratops. Brachiosaurus. Pterodactyl. Okay, you guys," I said. "Now each of you make a wish and blow out a candle." Their eyes lit up. After they blew out their candles, I led them in singing "Happy Birthday" to Mouse.

"Now you can eat your prehistoric ice cream," I said. "And whoever finds a gummy dinosaur in the bottom of his or her dish wins a prize."

"What is it?" piped Danny.

Mom looked at me and turned her palms up, indicating that she didn't have any prizes to give out.

"Don't worry," I mouthed. She looked puzzled.

Jason found the gummy dinosaur and shouted, "I got it! I got it!"

I pulled out a small package and handed it to Jason. He opened it. It was the little rubber brontosaurus. From the look on his face I could tell it was a big hit. Mom just stared. She was a little flabbergasted, I think.

We got a little silly after that, waiting for the parents to show up, but it wasn't anything like the chaos we'd walked in on. Becky had the kids laughing as she bounced balloons off their heads. Still in my clown suit, I tried a somersault, and soon Becky and the little kids were also tumbling across the living room.

Just as I was about to go into another somersault, with my rear end in the air, who do you think walked in? My sister Suzanne and her boyfriend,

Tommy Piper! Tommy always teases me, and that time was no exception.

"Bottoms up!" he said to me as he walked by.

I sat down fast, mortified. By the time I looked around, Tommy was gone. Becky tried to reassure me.

"Allie, what are you worried about?" she said. "Tommy didn't even know it was you. After all, it wasn't your *face* he saw!"

That got her laughing so hard she did another somersault. It was easy for her to make fun. Even though she's my best friend, at that moment I could have punched Becky right in her red clown nose.

Six

As parents arrived to pick up their kids, the squeals and giggles of happy children filled the room.

"Mommy! Look, Mommy!"

Kenny Dawson ran up to his mother, showing her his balloon.

"Hey, that's great!" said Mrs. Dawson. Mom told her it was Julie's idea and Rosie had done the artwork.

"Really?" said Mrs. Dawson. "I wish I'd had a couple of geniuses around when I had Kenny's party last month. The entertainer I hired wasn't very good with such young children. The kids were so bored they were ready to tear each other apart and then start in on my house! And I still had to order the cake and do the decorations and food myself."

Except for one last crisis, when Danny couldn't find his other shoe, things went smoothly. The shoe was finally discovered in the toy dump truck, where

Tracy Lewis had thoughtfully loaded it. At last all the parents and children were gone.

"Does anybody here like mocha?" asked Becky, breaking through the sudden quiet.

"Yes!" we answered all at once, and raced to the kitchen. It didn't take us long to find clean Happy New Year plates and forks, and soon we were sitting around the table devouring the rejected birthday cake.

"We earned this," I said, spearing a huge chunk.

"I thought we'd never get our cake," confessed Julie.

"Julie, how come you're so thin when you have such a humongous appetite?" asked Becky.

"I don't know," she said, displaying her silvery grin again. "My sisters call me the bottomless pit. They can't stand that I can eat and eat and eat and never gain weight while they're always on diets."

"Some people are just lucky, I guess," groaned Becky.

Mom walked in.

"You guys saved the day!" she said. "I'm so grateful to you for taking care of the kids. They loved you! I think they had a good time, don't you?"

"Oh, for sure!" said Rosie. "I know I did!"

"Ditto," said Becky.

"But it's only because of you four that it worked out," said Mom. "Believe me, it was not a pretty picture before that."

Dad came in and handed us each an envelope.

"What's this?" I asked.

"Look and see," said Dad.

There was a ten-dollar bill inside each envelope!

"But—" Becky began.

"No buts," said Mom.

We all looked at each other.

"Mrs. Gray," Becky said, "this is really nice of you, but we can't take your money."

"Why not?"

"Well, because we wanted to do it. We can't take money for that. It isn't right."

I felt like strangling Becky. *Why does she have to be so generous and thoughtful all the time?* I thought. *I could really use that money for my concert ticket!*

Mom and Dad exchanged glances with each other.

"That's really commendable," said Dad. "You're very fine people. But think of it this way: we would have paid the clown, but since you did his job the money's really yours. You earned it. Besides, we insist you keep it, okay?"

"That's so nice of you," said Rosie.

"Yes, it is. Thank you so much," said Julie.

"Wow. Thanks!" Becky chimed in. "Really!"

Before I could add my two (grateful) cents, the phone rang. Mom answered. I heard her say, "Oh, hi, Marilyn," and knew it was Becky's mother. We were all trying not to listen—or at least we were trying to listen without being too obvious about it—

to my mother tell Becky's mother about Mouse's party and how we saved the day. Becky, of course, wasn't even *pretending* not to listen. After all, it was Becky's mother on the phone and Becky figured that she was next in line to talk to her.

So it wasn't any great surprise a few minutes later when my mother handed Becky the phone.

We heard Becky squeak, "Really? That's great, Mom. I'll be right over."

"I got a job!" she told us as soon as she hung up. "My mom says there's a flood of guests tonight— something to do with the college because there are a lot of parents in town. So I'm going to keep the salad station stocked. And she's paying me! Three-fifty an hour!"

We all knew how long Becky had been hoping for just such a chance.

"Lucky!" said Julie.

"You're getting richer by the minute," my dad said. "You were meant to be wealthy. It has been ordained." He made a steeple out of his fingers and bowed at Becky. We all rolled our eyes, even Mom.

"Can you believe it, Allie?" Becky said. She was so excited. "My parents have actually asked me to work at the Moondance! For money, just like a regular employee."

"That's great," I said. I meant it, too, but I had mixed feelings. I mean, I can never earn extra money because all my babysitting is for my family, for free. Becky was so lucky to be able to earn some extra bucks right when she needed it. When *we* needed it. At this rate, Becky would be able to go to the concert and I'd have to stay home. It didn't seem fair.

"I've got to go!" yelped Becky. "I have to be there by five, looking normal. Can I wash my face here?"

"Of course," said Mom, dashing down the hall. She came back with cold cream and a box of tissues. She took off Becky's clown makeup and Rosie took off mine.

"We'll walk with you," Julie told Becky, putting on her jacket. Rosie followed. "We have to get going, anyway."

After they left, Mom came up to me.

"Allison, I'm really proud of you—in more ways than one," she added, giving me a hug. "How did you come up with so many good ideas, and that wonderful prize?" she asked.

I explained to her about losing the package and buying the miniature dinosaur, just in case.

"Your dad and I want to reimburse you for it," Mom said. "It was a party expense, and you shouldn't have to spend your own money on it."

Thanks to my parents, I was up to twelve dollars and change in my concert fund. I still didn't have enough for my ticket, but next week's allowance would give me four more dollars and if I didn't spend a single cent between now and then, that would leave me only two dollars short. Two dollars didn't seem like a lot. Surely I'd think of a way to earn two little old dollars by then.

I looked at the clown suit I'd thrown over my chair. In the rush, I'd forgotten to give it to Becky before she left. It suddenly occurred to me that while I had been acting like a clown, helping Becky with her magic, and singing with the children, not once had I stumbled over my words or felt as if there were a dry sponge in my throat. I hadn't been shy at all!

Seven

On Sunday, I planned to spend the entire day working on my report on the Mayan Indians. Normally I would have done it Friday night, maybe Saturday at the latest. But all the excitement over the Vermilion concert and Mouse's birthday had just blown it right out of my mind. I hate to leave anything, especially a school report, to the last minute, but there I was, just starting work on it.

Actually, I was staring at my desk while my mind wandered. Wouldn't it be great if I had a million dollars and I could buy anything I wanted whenever I wanted it? Concert tickets—front row center, of course—would be no problem. I could even hire a limousine to take me there in style.

Becky and I often thought about what we would do if we were billionaires. We both love animals, so we always figured that one thing we'd do for sure is give money to the Save the Animals Fund. Then maybe they could build a special home for all the orphaned pets and hire people to take care of them. And I'd be rich enough to be able to adopt a lot of them, too. I'd buy a house big enough so that every cat, every dog, and every parakeet would have its own room. And I'd have two swimming pools in my backyard. One would be for the dolphin and one would be for me and my friends. I could invite them over to swim anytime, even in cold weather, because there would be a plexiglass bubble over the pool and the temperature would always be just right—not too warm, not too cool.

In the middle of my daydream, I heard the phone ring. Then I heard my mom calling, "Allison, it's for you."

I ran downstairs to the kitchen, and Mom held out the receiver. "It's business," she said mysteriously. I took the phone.

"Hello?"

"Allison," said a voice, "this is Mrs. Plummer, Jason's mother. Mrs. Dawson told me that it was you and your friends who were responsible for Jonathan's party yesterday."

"Well, the clown couldn't make it, so we tried to fill in."

"Jason had a wonderful time. He hasn't stopped talking about it! And so I'm wondering if I could hire you and your friends to give a party for my daughter, Lisette. She's going to be six years old next week. I've already sent out the invitations, but

I haven't really thought about what I'm going to do. Is there enough time for you to plan something?"

"Well, I have to ask my friends," I told her. "Can I have your number, please?" I tore a page off the pad by the phone and rummaged frantically for a pencil. Of the four in the cup by the phone, only one had anything you could really call a point on it. (Why is it that if you can find a pad you can't find anything to write on it with? And vice versa?) I scribbled down Mrs. Plummer's number and promised to call her back later in the day.

The first thing I did, naturally, was call Becky. We're all best friends, like I said, but Becky and I are special best friends. We're practically twins, we're so close.

"Becky!" I nearly shouted into the phone.

"Allie, what's up?" Becky wasn't used to me bursting out like that.

"Uh, how did it go last night?" I'd almost forgotten to ask her about her job. The truth was, I didn't really want to know how great it had been and how much money she'd made. But I just couldn't talk to Becky without asking about it. Besides, she was my best friend, and part of me really did care and was happy for her.

"Fine. I made seventeen fifty and I didn't do anything weird or break anything. I only spilled one glass of water, and the lady was very nice about it. But I'm *soooo* tired today. I slept till ten o'clock!"

"Becky, guess what?" I couldn't hold the news in any longer.

When I told her about the party for Mrs. Plummer, she nearly plotzed. (That's a Yiddish expression, and it means "exploded." We learned it from Julie, who learned it from her grandmother Goldie, who says it all the time.)

"So what are we waiting for?" Becky exclaimed.

"You think we should do it?"

"Of course, you nut! It's the answer to our problems! The road to riches!"

That's the difference between me and Becky. While I'm still thinking over an idea and getting used to it, she runs ahead with it. She doesn't mind letting the whole thing fall into place as she goes. Me, I'm a planner.

"But. . . ."

"She'd pay us, right?"

"Right."

"Well, you call Rosie and I'll call Julie and we'll tell them to come over to the attic this afternoon. We'll ask them. If they say yes, well, the four of us will be in the party business."

Becky made perfect sense, of course. With four of us we'd be able to come up with tons of great ideas. We all liked little kids and were good with them. With all of us pitching in and working together, we'd make money and have a great time in the bargain. And I could definitely earn enough to see Vermilion!

"Allison? You sound funny. Are you okay?"

"Yeah. I guess I can't really b-b-believe that some-one w-would pay us money to give a party." I was so excited that my darn stammer came back. "We'd better call Rosie and Julie right away," I told Becky, "before I wake up and find out I'm dreaming."

We met in Becky's attic that afternoon at two o'clock. The attic was huge and airy and filled with lampshades, trunks, dressers, mirrors, even an old player piano. (The piano didn't work too well, though, and when we tried it out once it boomed so loudly through the Moondance that Becky's mother made us promise to leave it alone from then on.) Anyway, when Mrs. Bartlett told Becky that she could use the attic when her friends came over, Becky asked me to help clean it up. So one Saturday we pushed things aside so we could have a big space for ourselves in the middle, and we spread old rugs and pieces of carpeting over the creaky wooden floor-boards. We added old cushions donated by our families, and on the bare wood of the slanted ceiling we tacked some of our favorite posters. It really looked cool. It was like our own private clubhouse.

"Wow!" said Rosie after we'd told her about the party business idea. "When I said we were a great team, you guys really took me seriously, didn't you?" Rosie stretched out on the threadbare Oriental carpet, looking a little like Cleopatra with her olive skin and dark hair against the intricate, deep red floral design of the rug. She had long glossy pink nails, too, and I felt a twinge of jealousy. I'd never have nails like Rosie's because I chewed mine too much.

Becky chimed in. "Well, look at us. We're a perfect group for this business. We need someone who is organized: that's Allie. We need an artist: that's Rosie. We need someone who's enthusiastic and likes people: that's Julie. And me? I'll take care of the food."

Julie, in an aqua and grey football shirt and jeans, sat cross-legged on an old cushion. "I love parties," she said, "and kids. This is great. You guys are brilliant!"

"We can make up a flyer," said Rosie, "and distribute it so we can get more jobs! I'll design it." She rolled up the sleeves of her blouse, looking very businesslike, and pulled out her pad and pens.

"Great," said Becky. "But we need a name first. Any ideas?"

"How about Party People?" I suggested.

"Let's Have a Party?" offered Julie.

"No, too long. Not catchy."

"The Party Makers?" said Rosie.

"Not bad, but I don't know . . . maybe we can come up with something a little snappier." It went on like this for a while, with all of us tossing out names. Some of them got pretty silly, like Becky's idea to call the business Whoopie Do. Finally I just hit on it.

"What about The Party Line?" I asked.

"That's good!" said Becky.

"I like it," said Julie.

"I can already see a logo for it," said Rosie. "A telephone, with its cord curling across the page spelling out the name." She began sketching on her pad.

And that was it. So, officially, we called ourselves The Party Line, which would be a kind of club or business that planned parties. The four of us were partners.

We figured out the officers right away. Becky, of course, was president, because it was her idea to start the business. I was vice president, because I got the call from Jason's mom that started it all. Julie was secretary because the secretary takes notes at the meetings and she has neat handwriting. Rosie was our treasurer; she had to keep track of all the money we made (and spent). Rosie was best in math.

Julie borrowed a sheet of paper from Rosie and began to write things down. I saw her write The Party Line in big letters at the top, and then all our names with our official titles after each.

"What about rules?" I asked.

"I hate rules," Julie said promptly. "Do we have to have any?"

"Maybe just a few," said Rosie. "So we can keep organized."

"Okay. How about a rule that we meet once a week?" said Becky.

"Fine." Julie seemed relieved. That was a rule anybody could live with. But I bet she'd have agreed to anything just to get it over with.

"What about dues?" asked Rosie, playing with one of her nails.

"Why?" said Becky.

"Oh, to pay for running off the flyers on a copying machine, for example," Rosie answered.

"That's fair," said Becky. "But instead of dues, why don't we use part of the money we make? After all, the whole reason to be in business is to make money, not spend it. My allowance doesn't go far enough as it is."

"Okay. Enough rules for now?" Rosie asked.

"Yes!" said Julie emphatically. She drew a big exclamation point on the page.

"Yes!" I agreed. I wasn't too thrilled with a lot of rules, either.

We all agreed that ten percent of our fee—of our profit, really—would go into the treasury for expenses. Julie wrote it down.

"How do we know what to charge?" asked Rosie.

We looked at each other.

"Good question," said Becky.

"We can figure it out after we know how much

the client wants to spend, how many people are coming, what our supplies will cost, that kind of thing. We'll need some kind of information sheet to keep track of all the details. I'll make one up," I volunteered. I secretly loved doing things like that— making lists, getting organized on paper. It wasn't really much of a secret; all my friends knew what I was like.

"Good. I was hoping you'd say that, Allie," said Becky.

"Then we can look at the sheet and figure out our expenses, add on our profit, and tell the customer what the bottom line is," said Rosie. "We should ask for half the money in advance so we can buy party supplies."

Rosie was really the perfect treasurer. Not only is she good in math, but she has a head for finance. She sounded like a regular banker.

"That's a great idea, Rosie," said Julie. "And with four of us, getting everything done should be no problem." She looked at her notes. "Anyone have anything else to add?"

"I do," I said. "I've seen my parents doing parties for the kids in my family for a long time. There's a lot of work, even when you hire someone like a clown to come and entertain. I think if we're going to provide a really good party service, we should do it all, so the parents can relax."

"You mean, we'll do the decorations?" asked Julie. "And get the cake?"

"Yes, we'll even send invitations—whatever it takes. We'll do everything. All the parents have to do is provide the place to have the party."

"And pay us!" said Rosie.

"Right!"

"I love it," said Becky. "This is going to be fantastic."

"Uh-oh," said Rosie. We all looked over at her. I could hardly believe my eyes. Rosie was staring intently at one of her fingernails *and was pulling it off!*

"It was loose," she explained, looking up at me.

"What?" I cried. I was horrified.

"Allie, relax, they're fake nails," Julie put in.

"Yeah. You should try them, Allie," added Rosie. "They might help keep you from chewing on your own nails. That's one of the reasons I started wearing them."

I'd heard about fake nails, of course. I just never realized that Rosie wore them. "What's the other reason?" I asked.

Even Becky rolled her eyes at me now. "Because they look better, you dweeb! You know what a perfectionist Rosie is."

It was true. Rosie was a stickler about her appearance. I felt a little stupid, as if I hadn't seen something that was right under my nose until I tripped over it. But now that I thought about it, the idea of fake nails seemed fascinating.

"Back to business," Becky said briskly. "Allie, you'll call Jason's mother tonight and tell her we'll do the party, right?"

"Right," I said. "Talk to you later." I grabbed my jacket and bounded down the stairs. I couldn't wait to get home to work on the information sheet so we could get started. Outside, I broke into a run. I practically had my ticket in my hand. I was so happy I started to sing—quietly, it's true, and to myself, but still, singing out loud all the same.

Eight

"All-ison!"

It was suppertime. I had no idea it had gotten so late. And I'd been so busy I hadn't even started writing my Mayan report.

"Be right there!" I called. I brought the information sheet with me and left it by the phone in the kitchen.

While we ate I told my parents about The Party Line. Not that I got to tell them much. With a family the size of mine, someone's always talking. It seems as if we have about four conversations all going on at the same time.

As soon as we finished supper I made my telephone call. There was more than one advantage to getting out of doing the dishes. I could get my calls out of the way and get right to work on that report.

"Hello, Mrs. Plummer. This i-is Allison Gray. I-I'm calling about the p-party. . . ." I crossed my fingers and tried not to be nervous. I hated it when I stammered. For some reason, it always seemed worse on the phone.

"Ah, yes. What did your friends say?"

"Well, we talked about it, and if you ... um ... still want us, we'd be happy to do the party for Lisette." I stretched the phone cord to reach into the dining room so I could get away from the clatter of Suzanne's dishwashing and have a little privacy. Feeling as if I were in the middle of a construction site wasn't going to help my nervousness.

The information sheet made everything work smoothly. I asked Ms. Plummer questions and filled in the blanks as she gave me the answers. There would be eight children, boys and girls all around six years old. She wanted a birthday cake and all the trimmings. She didn't want to spend more than a hundred dollars. I promised to call her back as soon as we figured out how much we'd have to charge.

"Fine, fine," she said. "But you'll need some money to get started. I'll drop off twenty-five dollars in the morning on my way to work."

I was halfway through dialing Becky's number when my mom walked in.

"Allison, did you finish your schoolwork for tomorrow?"

"N-no. Not all of it."

"Then maybe you'd better get to it instead of making more phone calls. It's already eight o'clock, and it's a school night, you know."

"Okay, Mom."

I put the phone down and went upstairs. I'd see Becky on the bus tomorrow.

It was true I'd neglected the Mayan report over the weekend. Not only did I still have to write the final version, I had to make a report cover. Mr. Reed always liked my covers. If I didn't do a good one, he'd notice. He might not realize that a dull cover meant I hadn't left myself time to make a good one, but I would. Besides, I always looked forward to his compliments.

I chewed off two nails but I finally got my report written. As I read it over for the third time, my mom knocked and came in.

"How's it going?" she asked, putting a glass of milk and a plate with three oatmeal-raisin cookies on it on my desk. She peered at the report cover lying there. A gold foil sunburst lay on a folded sheet of black construction paper. Underneath, letters cut out of red and aqua paper spelled out The Mayan People.

"I saw you were still up. It's nearly eleven o'clock. Allison, I hope Jonathan's party wasn't the reason you neglected your schoolwork. If I had known . . . ."

"It wasn't that," I said, a little guiltily. "I got so excited about The Party Line, I just forgot about the time."

"Mmm," she said. "Okay. Try to finish soon so you can get some sleep." She leaned over and kissed me. "I like your cover."

After Mom left, I sipped the milk and put the finishing touches on my report cover. I really loved the Mayan culture; that was one of the most interesting projects we had ever had to do. I was glad I hadn't blown it.

It was late when I finally got into bed, though. As soon as my head hit the pillow I was out like a light.

Nine

On the school bus the next morning Becky and I were trying to work out what party supplies we'd need and how much they'd cost.

"What about the cake?" I asked.

Becky's eyes lit up, which was unusual for her so early in the morning. "I *knew* there was something I had to tell you," she said excitedly.

Just then Rosie got on. "Hi!" she greeted us. "What's the latest on our party business?"

"As I was *saying*," Becky said in a mock-stern voice, looking pointedly at Rosie, who stuck out her tongue, "I have some great news. The baker who does the desserts for the Moondance said he'd give us the same forty percent discount he gives the restaurant."

I must've looked surprised, because she explained, "Well, he made a delivery yesterday, so I asked him."

Leave it to Becky. She just barrels ahead on everything.

"Anyway," Becky continued, "He can make us a cake, any flavor, for only seven-fifty! He'll even throw in the birthday candles!"

"Hey, that's great!" I said. Rosie gave Becky a thumbs-up sign.

I pulled out the information sheet and wrote "$7.50" in the space under Expenses.

Rosie leaned over my shoulder. "What's that?"

"The information sheet," I replied, showing it to her. "What do you think?"

"I like it," said Rosie. "Very businesslike."

"Oh, here's something else," I said, handing her the envelope with the money that Mrs. Plummer had dropped off that morning.

"Wow!" said Rosie. "We really *are* in business." She took the money and carefully stowed it away in her backpack.

The bus reached its next to last stop, and Julie bounced on. She seemed really impressed with my information sheet, and that made me feel good. If everybody liked it, then all the time I spent on it was worth it.

"We ought to decide on a theme for Lisette's party," said Becky.

"I've never met Lisette," I said, "but I know her brother Jason. He was at Mouse's party. If she's six years old, we can do nursery rhymes or fairy tales. They're both pretty popular with that age group."

"What about storybook characters? We could tell each child to dress up as his or her favorite character." That was Rosie.

"Yes!" said Becky. "And *we* can dress up, too!"

"I love it!" said Julie. "This is going to be fun. If I can find my green tights, I'll be Robin Hood."

"I'll have to tell Mrs. Plummer about the costumes," I said. "I can do that when I call her with the price."

"Right. Better do it tonight, since the party is this Saturday."

I clutched. *Saturday!* Could we get everything done in just five days? I tried not to panic.

"Let's go to the store this afternoon and check prices so we can figure out our costs," said Becky. "I'll order the cake tomorrow, and we'll walk home from school Friday and shop for party things. Okay?"

"Good idea," said Rosie.

Becky's plan immediately calmed me down. Having four of us to figure things out certainly made life a lot easier.

Julie was looking at the information sheet again.

"What about music?" she asked. "I'm sure among the four of us we have plenty of good tapes. I'll make a special tape for the party, and we can bring my portable cassette player."

"I can borrow some of Mouse's tapes, too." I offered. "Then we can mix fun music with kiddie songs."

Julie nodded enthusiastically.

I penciled in "music" on the information sheet.

Everyone was excited about our first official job. Whoever said Mondays were blah? I was in a great mood.

Once we got to school, my good mood ended with a big thump.

"You will be having a midterm a week from Friday," our biology teacher, Ms. Pernell, announced, "covering the year's work to date. Diagrams, experiments, theories, projects, the works." We groaned loudly, but it didn't change anything.

At least in social studies Mr. Reed beamed at me. "Terrific cover, Allison," he said as he placed my report on top of the pile on his desk.

The rest of the day sped by quickly. I could hardly wait until school ended so we could get started on our party shopping. That afternoon we zipped through the supermarket and made a checklist: napkins, paper plates, plastic cups. We moved to another aisle and did the same for soda and candy.

We all had to get home to study, and Rosie had two hours of piano practice as well, so I offered to add up the costs on my own. Since everyone knows I'm pretty lame when it comes to math, they seemed relieved to know that I was planning to rely on a calculator.

While I was figuring it all out, Julie called. She was excited.

"My dad says he'll run off copies of our flyer, when we have it, on the copier at his office. I was thinking, though, that we should probably wait until after the midterm, huh?"

Julie hardly ever worried about schoolwork, but the midterm was a pretty big deal.

"Sure," I told her, relieved not to be the only one worrying about schoolwork. "It can wait. I'll call Rosie and let her know."

I phoned Rosie and then went back to my party calculations. By the time I'd finished and added on a few extra dollars (just in case) for things we might have forgotten, the total came to nearly fifty dollars.

"Is that all?" said Mrs. Plummer when I called her. "That sounds very reasonable to me. I'll drop off the rest of the money tomorrow morning. And the idea for the storybook characters theme is charming. I'll call the other parents right away."

After dinner Becky called to talk about our costumes. She was trying to come up with some storybook characters that worked in pairs, like Tweedledum and Tweedledee, so we could plan our costumes together.

So far so good. Except there wasn't much time left for studying that night, after all the phone calls.

I didn't want to panic again, so for the rest of the evening, what little was left of it, I put aside everything else and became deeply absorbed in the wonders of the pancreas.

Ten

"Why does my diagram look like chickens have marched all over it with muddy feet while yours looks like a book illustration?" groaned Becky on the school bus the next morning.

"Try using colored pencils to keep the organs separate from one another. It really helps." I showed her my red and blue pencils.

"You're so organized!" she said. "It's the same thing with The Party Line information sheet. It should hang in a museum. We'd have a hard time getting our act together if it weren't for you."

"I have to be organized, Beck," I told her. "In my family, if I didn't keep track of things I'd never be able to find anything. I guess it just spills over into other parts of my life." What Becky didn't realize is that it was as much her ideas as my organization that kept us going.

When Rosie got on the bus I handed her an envelope.

"More money?" she asked. "Already?"

I nodded. "That's the other twenty-five dollars. We're charging Ms. Plummer a total of fifty dollars. She dropped this off this morning."

"Did you get your practicing in yesterday?" Becky asked Rosie.

"Yes," said Rosie. "But I barely had time for anything else."

"I know what you mean," I said. "I was on the phone so much yesterday that the evening was almost gone before I got around to homework."

We waved to Julie as she got on the bus.

"I have another problem besides time," confessed Rosie. "My parents want me to try and stick to only one or two calls a night. What if something really important comes up? I may not be able to talk to all of you."

"Well, my parents like me to limit my phone time to between eight and nine o'clock," said Becky. That wasn't news to me. I was used to Becky's telephone hour from way back in second grade.

"My parents complain about us tying up the phone," Julie said, picking up on our conversation in the middle. "But they don't ever really stop me from using it. With my sisters and me, I think my parents consider it a losing battle." Julie's two sisters were older and dated a lot. "The only problem is that our phone is always busy."

"How are we going to do Party Line business if we have all these different phone rules?" I asked.

We all thought about this for a minute.

"I have an idea!" Naturally, it was Becky who came up with a plan.

We all perked up. "So tell us," said Rosie.

"First, on the bus in the morning we can have short meetings. If there's any new party business to discuss, we can probably get most of it taken care of then."

"Right," said Julie. "I'm with you so far."

"Okay," Becky continued. "Then we can have real meetings on weekends, in the attic. But when something comes up between meetings that's too important to wait, we can make a telephone chain."

"What's that?" I asked.

"One person calls another, and that person calls the next, until we all have the message. Get it? It's like a chain. Then each of us only has to make one phone call, which shouldn't take too long. And—ta-da—we can make our chain call between eight and nine o'clock!"

"Maybe I can convince my sisters to stay off the phone for that hour," said Julie.

Becky had done it. She had figured out a way around our problems, as usual. She was amazing.

"How will we know who to call?" I asked.

"Let's put our initials into a hat and each pick

someone out," said Becky. "Whoever you pick, that's who you'll call."

Rosie pulled out a pen and a sheet of paper. In each corner, she wrote one of our initials. She tore the paper into four pieces, folded them carefully and put them in the top of her lunchbag.

"I don't have a hat," she explained with a shrug.

Julie pulled my name, I pulled Becky's, Becky pulled Rosie's, and Rosie pulled Julie's.

The invention of the telephone chain took care of some of our problems. If only it could have done my homework, too.

The rest of the week it would have been almost impossible to tell that we were in the party business, except that we tested the chain and talked over some details of Lisette's party. The chain worked! We were able to keep party plans going without spending all our time on the phone about it.

When the last bell rang on Friday, we burst out of school as though we had been held captive for a week by terrorists. Our first stop was Becky's, where we dropped off our stuff. Then we headed for the mall, of course.

"Look." Becky stopped in front of a new store called The Perfect Party. We looked in the windows. They were filled with colorful displays of hats and noisemakers, streamers and confetti, and all kinds of party favors and decorations. Last week there had been just a big sign out front that said Opening Soon. Not only had they acted pretty fast, but their timing was perfect. What a great place to open just as we were starting up a party business!

"They have everything we need in one place, and it's all for parties!" said Julie.

We went inside. At the door, we picked up a bright pink enameled shopping basket.

"Look, aren't these cute?" said Julie, holding up a package of paper plates. Printed on them were the words Birthday Girl and a picture of an adorable little raccoon in a pink party dress surrounded by laughing raccoons wearing party hats and blowing noisemakers.

"They look like storybook characters," said Becky.

"We need eight," I reminded her. There were exactly eight plates in the package. Becky tossed them in the basket and Julie found matching napkins and cups.

Next Julie picked up a big wax candle shaped like a number six. "This is perfect, isn't it?"

"Isn't the baker giving us free candles?" asked Rosie.

"Yes," said Becky, taking it from Julie and dropping it into the basket. "But it would really make our first party look professional. We could use both."

Rosie clicked her tongue. "Let's try not to spend more than we have in the treasury, okay? If the baker is giving us candles, let's pass this up."

Becky reluctantly put the candle back on the shelf, but exploded with delight a second later when she discovered toys and party favors.

"Balloons!" she cried. She threw two packages of multicolored balloons with Happy Birthday printed on them into the basket. I was holding the basket, which kept getting heavier and heavier.

"Hey, take it easy." I said. "My arm is going to break."

The truth was, I had a feeling I had forgotten something, but I couldn't think what. We certainly needed plates and cups and balloons, but I wished we had made up a list. That was what I'd forgotten: the checklist we'd made up on Monday. I would have felt better if I could see the list and check items off as we went along.

Finally we picked out two plastic toys to give as game prizes and a pin the nose on the clown game.

"Well, at least we can use this game again for the next party," said Rosie.

At the checkout counter, Rosie and I stood together in front as the salesperson rang up each purchase. We'd look at the cash register ring up another amount, and we'd look at each other. We were definitely thinking the same thing: it looked like a lot of dollars and cents adding up. The total bill, with tax, came to twenty-nine dollars and sixty-four cents.

'Oh, no!" I cried. The salesperson frowned, and Rosie quickly reassured her.

"That's okay," she said. "We have the money." She opened the envelopes from Mrs. Plummer and took out three ten-dollar bills.

As we left the store, Julie turned to us. "We still need soda and candy. What do you say, the supermarket next?"

"Yup." Becky seemed completely unconcerned. Maybe Rosie and I were just being worrywarts.

At the store Rosie checked prices while Becky loaded our cart with all kinds of soda—regular colas and cherry-berry flavors, too. We bought bags and bags of different kinds of candy for the goody bags. Finally we added a couple of big bags of potato chips and pretzels.

The checker rang it up, and it came to twelve dollars and seventy-three cents.

"I can't believe it," I said to Becky. "We're way over our estimate."

Becky frowned. "I don't think the prices we figured out on Monday were the same as in the party store. Rosie was right to worry."

"We also added a lot of things that weren't on the list," Rosie reminded her.

"Well, it's too late to change things now. We don't have time."

We went back to Becky's and went up to the attic to rest our tired legs for a while.

I sat on the floor looking at the information sheet, which I'd left behind in my backpack. I kept going over the figures. How could we be so broke so fast? At last it hit me.

"Hey, everybody," I said, feeling extraordinarily dumb. "I think I'd b-better tell you s-something." There was silence, and I could feel everyone's eyes on me.

"What's up?" asked Rosie. "Whatever it is, Allie, it's nothing to look so worried about."

"Yes, it is," I said miserably. "The reason we're almost out of money is because I forgot to add our p-profit into the p-price I gave Mrs. P-plummer."

I heard a chorus of groans. "And we still have to pay for the cake tomorrow," Becky added.

Rosie shrugged. "What's done is done."

"I'm sorry," I said. "I really messed up."

"Hey, we all did, Allie," said Julie. "We'll just have to make up for it next time. It's a good experience."

"It's experience. Period." Becky said wryly.

"Look, it's no big deal," said Rosie. "We're just better at parties than we are at being businesspeople. But, Allie, let's remember to add a line for Profit to the information sheet next time."

"That's for sure!" I said. All that work for nothing! Everyone was being so nice that I didn't want to look as awful as I felt and spoil it. I tried to concentrate on the party tomorrow. We had to do a great job. Our reputation, and future jobs, depended on it.

Walking home, Rosie had a great idea. "We ought

to take pictures," she said, "so we can show potential customers what our parties look like. We can put the pictures in a book and show it to people."

"Who has a camera?" I asked.

"I do," said Rosie. "I'll bring it."

"We should pay you for the film and the developing, though," I said. "And we don't have any money in the treasury right now, because what's left has to go toward the cake."

"That's okay." Rosie smiled at me. "I already have some film in my camera. We'll worry about the developing later."

Everyone was taking our money disaster really well, but I couldn't help thinking that it was all my fault we'd ended up in such a fix. Not only that, I'd blown my last chance to raise money for my concert ticket. I knew just as well as everyone else that the cake might cost more money than we had left. We were probably going to *lose* money. There was no way I'd get to the concert now.

Eleven

Julie and Rosie had already festooned the party
room with pink and silver streamers when Becky
and I arrived at the Plummers'. Julie, all in green
as Robin Hood, was blowing up balloons.

"Hi!" she called to us between breaths.

"You look terrific," cried Mrs. Plummer as she
helped us off with our coats. Becky and I were
dressed in matching outfits as Hansel and Gretel—
Becky's idea, of course.

Jason came running up to me to show me his Don-
ald Duck mask.

"Who could this be?" I asked in mock surprise.

Jason pulled the mask off. "It's me!" he shouted
triumphantly.

"Oh, Jason, you really fooled me!" He raced off,
giggling madly.

"It really looks fantastic, you guys," I said.

"It sure does," Becky agreed.

"Thanks," said Rosie. She was sitting on the floor

in a witch costume, cutting pink and silver paper strips. She grinned to expose a wad of black gum over her front teeth that made her look toothless.

Once she'd finished making the strips, Rosie used them to cover one of the dining room chairs. On the back of the chair was a piece of pink paper with Lisette's name written across it in silver glitter. I put a box of party decorations on the floor next to Rosie.

"Your lettering is perfect!" I told her.

"Thanks! What's in the box?"

"Leftovers from parties we've had at my house: crepe paper, Happy Birthday garlands, hats. I thought maybe we could use some of them."

"Great idea." Rosie said. "Would you take a look at the birthday chair and tell me if you think it needs anything else?"

"What about big silver stars?"

"Allie, you are the best. That's just the thing!"

Rosie handed me a roll of aluminum foil and a pair of scissors. I knelt down and began cutting out star shapes, glad to have something to do. Besides, I loved doing party decorations.

Becky had taken charge in the kitchen, getting the cake ready with candles in place and making up goody bags. The children would start arriving at one-thirty and would stay until four. It was already one o'clock.

Julie hung clusters of balloons from doorknobs and

mirrors in the dining room and even hung a bunch from the front door knocker. "This way, everyone will know right away where the party is," she explained.

Then Becky set the dining room table with a paper birthday tablecloth, the raccoon plates, cups, and napkins, forks, and the goody bags, which she'd tied with pink and blue ribbons.

The doorbell rang. We all looked at each other and gulped. Becky opened the door.

"Michael is the big bad wolf," his mom told us. Michael's face was smudged with black and his eyebrows were penciled into big dark bushy shapes. He wore a plastic wolf's nose on a string around his head.

"What a wonderful nose you have!" said Rosie.

"The better to thmell you with," said Michael, his voice muffled by the wolf's nose. We all laughed.

The doorbell rang again almost immediately. It was Emery, or rather the scarecrow from *The Wizard of Oz*. Real straw stuck out of his pants legs and shirt sleeves.

Pamela arrived with her father minutes later, adding Little Red Riding Hood to our cast of storybook characters. She wore a red cape with a hood and carried a little basket.

Joelle was Curious George, and Franklin wore white pants with a white T-shirt and a small blue jacket. If it weren't for the rabbit ears he wore, it might have been a little hard to tell he was Peter Cottontail.

By quarter of two, we also had Max from *Where the Wild Things Are* (this was Lisette's little brother, Jason) and Paddington Bear (Jeffrey). All the parents had gone, and the party was in full swing.

To start things out, we played Once Upon a Time. It was a version of the game where you start a story and someone else has to continue it, but we played it using only familiar storybook characters.

"Snow White was walking down the street one day, and she met the Three Little Pigs. 'Where are you going?' she asked. 'We're going to the . . . .' " Julie stopped in the middle of her sentence and pointed to Lisette.

"We're going to the circus!" said Lisette.

"Good!" said Julie. "And at the circus, what will we see?" She pointed at Emery.

Emery picked it up beautifully. "We'll see everyone standing on their heads!"

The children howled with glee at this.

When it was Joelle's turn, Julie couldn't get her to say anything.

"Where did the Three Little Pigs go then, Joelle?" she coaxed.

Joelle shook her head and looked as though she might cry.

"Don't you want to help tell the story?" Rosie said, trying to help. She put her arm around her. Joelle immediately burst into tears. Poor Rosie didn't know what to do.

I went over and whispered, "It's okay, Joelle. If you don't want to tell the story, you can just listen. Don't be sad. It's a funny story. Listen. It will make you laugh." Joelle stopped crying. The game went on without a hitch, skipping Joelle each time. She never actually laughed, but she did smile.

"What did I do?" asked Rosie afterward.

"Nothing," I assured her. "I just recognized shyness when I saw it. It think she's afraid to talk in front of so many people."

Next we brought in seven chairs for a game of musical chairs.

"There's a prize for the winner," said Becky.

Julie, in charge of the cassette player, started and stopped the music until there was only one chair and two children left: Jeffrey and Pamela. At last the music stopped, and Jeffrey pounced. But Pamela pounced harder, winning a wind-up chicken that hopped across the table and pecked.

"It's Chicken Little," said Becky, reminding everyone of our storybook theme.

We never got to play pin the nose on the clown because Julie played one of the kiddie song tapes and I started singing. I didn't even think about it; I just did it. I guess I was just having a good time. I encouraged the children to sing along with me, and before I knew it we were all swaying and clapping and having a great time, sitting on the floor together and going through all the favorites.

"Old MacDonald had a farm . . . ."

"E-I-E-I-O," they sang.

"And on this farm he had some . . . ."

"Cows!" shouted Jason.

There followed a chorus of moos that filled the room.

At two o'clock Becky made an announcement: "It's time for the costume parade, everyone. Get in line and follow Robin Hood. The best costume wins a prize!"

Julie played "Follow the Yellow Brick Road" from *The Wizard of Oz.* The children marched happily around the dining room table, chanting the words. Julie could just as easily have been the Pied Piper as Robin Hood in her green tights. Eventually she stopped the parade and the kids took seats around the table. They immediately emptied their goody bags and started munching. Lisette, as Cinderella, sat on the birthday chair, sucking on a huge red jawbreaker that made her lips impossibly pink.

"Lisette, you look pretty as a picture," said Rosie. Lisette beamed. "In fact—" Rosie dashed out of the room and returned with her camera. "Smile, Lisette." *Click!* Rosie winked at me.

Rosie, Julie, Becky, and I were the costume judges, of course. It was a tough choice to make, but we ended up giving the prize to Joelle. As Curious

George she wore a brown leotard with a long brown tail on back and a little brown cap with two pink paper ears sticking out above. When she first walked in she had been holding a banana, but that had been abandoned some time ago. Rosie took another picture, this time of Joelle as she got her prize, a paperback book of favorite fairy tales. Joelle smiled shyly at the camera, book in one hand and tail in the other.

Then I drew the curtains as Becky came in with a large chocolate birthday cake aglow with candles. Pink icing spelled out Happy Birthday Lisette. Rosie snapped a picture of the cake to add to her growing collection of party pictures.

While the children were digging into their cake, Mrs. Plummer came over.

"Allison, you have such a lovely voice," she said. "Are you taking singing lessons?"

"Um, no, not really." I was surprised by the idea. "I'd like to, but . . . I'm . . . I usually don't sing in front of people," I stammered.

Mrs. Plummer patted my shoulder. "Well, you really should. You sing well enough to be on stage!"

For the second time in a week I realized that while I had been singing for the kids I hadn't once stumbled over my words or felt self-conscious.

Once the cake was finished the children were ready for more fun and games. Becky declared that it was balloon time, and showed them how to balance balloons on their noses. Soon they were all staggering around, balloons bouncing off their faces. They bumped into one another and fell giggling in heaps on the floor.

When the party was nearly over, Rosie made the last announcement: "It's present time." We brought the birthday chair into the living room, and Lisette opened her presents one by one, squealing with delight at each.

"Now Lisette has presents for everybody," said Mrs. Plummer, coming in with an armload of small, cheerful-looking packages wrapped with bright paper and crinkly ribbon. She put them in front of Lisette, who handed them out to her friends.

As the children literally tore into their gifts, we all looked at each other and nodded. This was a great idea, and maybe next time we'd budget this into our estimate. The children seemed thrilled with what they uncovered, too. Each got a small book of stickers featuring different Disney characters.

As the parents arrived and one by one ushered their children out, Franklin's mother stopped to talk to Rosie.

"I understand you took some pictures?" Rosie nodded. "Well, I was wondering if I could buy copies from you. The children look so adorable in their costumes."

Another parent overheard and before long, most of them had requested prints. Rosie seemed surprised but pleased, and asked interested parents to write their names and phone numbers on a piece of paper.

Finally we were back where we started again: the four of us, Lisette, Jason, and Mrs. Plummer.

"We made it!" said Becky.

"Is there any cake left?" asked Julie.

"Julie!" Rosie cried.

"What?" Julie asked innocently. She couldn't help it if she was a traveling stomach.

"That's okay," said Mrs. Plummer, smiling. "There's plenty of cake left, and you've really earned it. Help yourselves."

We balanced our slices on napkins and sat on the floor to eat.

"This seems to be a tradition," said Becky.

"What? Pigging out on birthday cake after a party is over?"

"Well, it's not the worst idea you've ever had, Julie," said Rosie.

Twelve

"Well, I'd say our first party was a success." Becky sat on an old rag rug, her knees drawn up and her legs crossed at the ankles. In her purple polo shirt and purple leggings, she looked like a grape.

"Agreed," said Rosie, plumping a pillow.

I grabbed my favorite patchwork cushion and settled down on the attic floor.

"Well, I don't know." Julie sat cross-legged on a braided mat, blowing a pink bubblegum bubble to match the pink pillow on her lap. "Is it really a success if we didn't make any money?"

"Good question," Becky said. "Let's go over finances, okay?" We nodded in agreement. "We got fifty dollars from Ms. Plummer, and we spent forty-two dollars and thirty-seven cents. That leaves seven dollars and sixty-three cents.

Julie opened a bag of corn chips and passed them around.

"Don't forget," Becky continued, "we owe my parents seven-fifty for the birthday cake."

I groaned. Thirteen cents wasn't much of a profit. And after we split it four ways—well, if I didn't feel so sorry for myself I probably would have thought it was funny.

We decided to leave the thirteen cents in the treasury. "Maybe it will multiply when we're not looking," said Julie, giggling. "Like the hamster in second grade, remember?"

I laughed, but my heart wasn't really in it.

"Okay, let's move on," said Becky. "Rosie had a great idea, taking pictures. All the parents want copies, and it's a good way to make extra money."

"True," I said, "but if Rosie wants to do it, then she should keep the money. It was her idea, and she used her own camera and film, too."

"Wait a second!" said Rosie. "The Party Line can buy the film and pay for the developing, and I'll take the pictures, but I think the money should go into the treasury. Who knows? Maybe the pictures will get us more jobs. And if we get more jobs, we'll make more money. Besides, I wouldn't be able to sell copies of the pictures if it weren't for The Party Line doing the party."

"Sounds good to me," said Becky. "But how will we pay for the film and the developing? It's bound to cost more than thirteen cents."

"The film was already in the camera," said Rosie.

"I had to finish the roll anyway, okay? And we'll pay the developing with the money the parents give us for the copies. I'll find out what they'll cost, add a little extra for some profit, and let everyone know."

"Thanks, Rosie," said Julie. Becky and I smiled our agreement. She was really being a good sport about this whole thing.

"By the way," I said, "we should remember to replace Rosie's art supplies when we *do* get money in the treasury. She used all her own glitter for the lettering." Rosie started to say something, but I just went ahead anyway. "And I *know* how expensive the glitter is. We've all heard Rosie talk about it." This was true and Rosie knew it.

"Well, I guess it's my turn to say thanks, Allie," she said.

"What I want to know is," said Julie, "how do we know what to charge for a job so we end up making money?"

"Well, look at this revised information sheet," I said as I handed a copy around. "See the last line? 'Profit: add fifty percent of total expenses.' "

"Really?" asked Rosie. "Fifty percent seems like a lot."

"I asked around," I said. "My parents asked a friend of their who owns a flower shop how she figures her profit. She said it works out to about fifty percent over costs.

"And my parents said that's about right in the restaurant business, too," added Becky.

"Hurray!" Julie applauded. "This is more like it! Now all we need are more parties to do." She looked at Rosie. "How's the flyer coming along?"

Rosie pulled a sheet of paper out of her pocket, unfolded it, and passed it to Julie.

"I was going to use a picture of the white rabbit from *Alice in Wonderland* and say 'Call us before it's too late,' but then I decided the smiling telephone was more fun. What do you think?"

In the top left corner of the flyer was a sketch of a telephone with a big smile under the pushbuttons. Rosie had drawn the phone cord curling across the top of the page so that it formed the words The Party Line. The cord continued down the right side of the flyer, and in the bottom right corner she'd sketched a receiver with the words *For the perfect party, call us* printed so they looked as if they were coming out of the receiver.

"That's great!" I said. It really did look good.

"I'd hire us, wouldn't you?" said Becky.

"You bet," said Julie. "It's perfect, Rosie."

Rosie smiled, leaning back on her hands. "I'll finish it tonight. I'm so glad you all like the design."

"And if my dad runs them off this week," said Julie, "we can distribute them over the weekend. Allie, he'll run off copies of the information sheet, too."

"Great. Then I can keep them in a looseleaf binder and we can use them to plan from party to party. We can keep it here in the attic."

"That's smart," said Rosie. "Then we can look up the costs of things from other parties so we can make estimates for potential customers."

We hung around for a while after that, finishing the corn chips and playing Becky's newest album. But the meeting was pretty much over. Because I live closer, I didn't have to leave as early as Rosie and Julie.

While they were clumping down the stairs and I was thinking I should be leaving pretty soon, too, Becky turned to me. "Look, Allie," she said. "I've been thinking. It's not as important for me to see Vermilion, and I have lots of extra money from my Moondance job." Suddenly she pushed a wad of money into my hand. "You can get a really great seat with this."

"No way!" I said, pushing the money back at her.

"Why not?" Becky was honestly surprised.

"Because, you goof, we're in this together. I don't *want* to go without you!"

"But—"

"No, Becky. I really appreciate it, but I can't go without you. You're my best friend. It wouldn't be any fun by myself." I gave Becky a hug. "You're a nut. Besides, I haven't given up all hope yet. I *might* get the money in time—you never know." Becky looked skeptical, but she knew I wouldn't change my mind. "I gotta go, Beck."

When I got home, Caroline was downstairs watching a nature special on television with the rest of the family. At last I had the room she and I shared all to myself. I put in a Vermilion tape and started dancing. I wanted to practice a step she did in her latest video. I thought I finally had it right. I pulled a scarf out of my dresser and let it fly around me as I moved, just like Vermilion does. It looked pretty and it felt cool. I looked in the little mirror over my dresser while I sang the words. I had it just right!

The phone rang. I ran downstairs to the kitchen with my scarf whipping straight out behind me. Mike was getting a snack out of the refrigerator and turned around just as I whizzed by. He got a mouthful of scarf.

"Allie, sometimes you are too weird!" He shook his head and left.

Mrs. Plummer was calling.

"Allison," she said, "I've been thinking about the party. You couldn't have charged me enough. Certainly not enough to have made money for yourselves. You spent about fifty dollars just in supplies alone."

"Um . . ." I didn't know what to say. She was right, but I didn't want to admit it.

"That's okay, Allie. I understand. I pushed you to do the party, and you were in a rush and didn't charge me enough. And now you're too nice to go back on your word. Well, I just don't feel right, and I'm dropping off another forty dollars tomorrow. No buts."

"Oh, Mrs. Plummer, you don't have to do that."

"Nonsense," she said briskly. "What's fair is fair, and you all did a wonderful job. If you don't make enough money, you may go bankrupt, and *then* where would I be? After all, Jason will be having a birthday soon, too."

I had to smile at Mrs. Plummer's cheerful insistence on setting things right. There was no question about it: Mrs. Plummer was a satisfied customer. I dialed Becky's number and told her the good news. She was thrilled to hear that we'd make a profit after all.

"And you know what else, Beck?" I began.

"Now you'll have enough for your ticket!" Becky laughed. "When are we going to the box office?"

"Well, I think my mom would lend me the money until tomorrow, and I bet she'd drive us over now. How soon can you be ready?"

"I'm already outside on my steps, waiting!"

The Taylor College theater lobby was empty. Colorful posters of Vermilion in scenes from her videos hung on the walls around the ticket booth. Becky and I ran up to the window.

"Two, please, as close to the stage as possible," I

said, practically out of breath. We put our money down.

"Sorry, but the concert is sold out."

"What?" My mouth fell open. "It . . . it can't be!"

"We sold the last ticket a week ago. Vermilion is pretty popular, you know."

I heard Becky saying "Oh, Allie," in a sad voice that sounded very far away. I felt tears coming and raced out of the theater before they spilled over.

When we got back in the car, Becky explained everything to my mom. I just stared out the window.

Thirteen

"Come on, Allie. You should know the answer to that one without even thinking." Becky was tossing questions at me from her biology notes as we bounced along on the school bus.

"Oh, I just wish this stupid midterm was over. It's all anyone thinks about anymore! I'm tired of it."

"Allie, what's with you?" asked Becky. "We have an exam to pass."

"Relax, Becky."

"How can I relax? You haven't studied with me once this week, and now it looks as if you haven't been doing it by yourself either. It just makes me worry all the more about how we'll do."

"I'll be fine. Have you ever known me to do badly on a major test? You'll see. Look." I took out my red and blue pencils. "I'm all set."

Becky closed her notebook and sighed. Suddenly I felt bad about how I'd been acting.

"Honestly, Becky, I'll do fine and so will you. The way you've been barking questions at me, I know you know this stuff."

Becky was right, though. When I walked into Ms. Pernell's classroom that morning, the reality of what was happening hit me like a brick in the face. I was not prepared for that test! Me, Allison Gray, who always got excellent grades! I was biting on a fingernail when Rosie passed my desk.

"You're nervous?" she whispered. "With your grades? Then how do you think I feel? I don't have butterflies in my stomach, I have pterodactyls."

I tried to smile confidently, but inside I was feeling less and less ready to take that exam. My colored pencils weren't much of a comfort.

For the next hour pencils scratched and papers rustled, but otherwise the room was quiet. You could almost hear the wheels turning in everyone's heads. Except mine. I came up blank on three out of four of the essay questions, and I knew I had blown some of the true/false, too. My palms were sweaty, and it wasn't even a warm day.

When the bell rang we shot out of Ms. Pernell's class and into the lunchroom, where the four of us compared notes. I'd been dreading this part, too.

I pretended I felt good about my answers, but I could hardly swallow my lunch. The rest of the day

I walked through classes like a zombie until I got to Mr. Reed's class.

"You did a fine job on these," he told us as he handed back our reports on ancient civilizations.

When mine got to me I was almost afraid to look. But when I did I almost yelled with pure joy. Across the top was a big A+ with a note in the margin from Mr. Reed: "I'm pleased with the depth of your understanding of this fascinating ancient culture, Allison." There was still hope for me.

"Allie," said Becky that afternoon, before getting off the school bus, "my mom asked me to work at the Moondance again tonight. You know, chopping veggies and things. Want to come over and help? I'll split my pay with you."

"Well . . . ." It wasn't the most exciting offer, but I didn't have anything else to do.

"Bring your pajamas and sleep over, too."

It would be fun. Besides, I loved being at the Moondance, even in the back. "Okay, thanks."

The restaurant was filling up, and it was only six o'clock. Usually it didn't get busy till later, so there must have been something going on at the college. Russell was busy cooking, and Becky's mom was showing people to their tables. The two waiters and three waitresses were all from the college. David was busing tables—keeping water glasses filled, clearing off empty plates, that sort of thing.

Becky and I tried to stay out of everyone's way. We were way in the back, behind some plants. We could see into the dining room pretty well. I had to turn around, but Becky was facing that way so she could keep an eye out in case someone needed something.

I was slicing a mushroom when I heard a deep, throaty voice somewhere behind me. I couldn't believe it.

"Vermilion!" I gasped. I could tell by the look on Becky's face that I was right. I put my knife down. "Becky, tell me everything. What's happening?"

"Mom's showing her to a table. It's number four, by the window. She's with this nice-looking man who's a lot older than she is."

I couldn't stand it anymore and turned to look just as David placed a basket of rolls on her table. It really *was* Vermilion, right here in the Moondance. Becky moved over, and I joined her on her side. I had to see everything.

Vermilion was reading the menu. When she looked up to order, I saw her violet-blue eyes. The man she was with ordered a drink, and they started talking.

I know it's rude to eavesdrop, but honestly, I

couldn't help it. I strained to hear every word. Unfortunately I could only hear a word here and there, so it was very frustrating. I knew what she ordered, though: poached salmon, salad with house dressing, and rice pilaf. The guy she was with had prime rib.

It seemed like hours might have passed while Vermilion and her friend finished dinner. But I was mesmerized. I could have watched her eat forever.

When coffee was served, Becky's mom brought it to the table herself. I saw her lean down and murmur something to Vermilion, and I saw Vermilion's extraordinary eyes widen as she listened. Becky's mom was probably telling her how happy they were that she'd visited the Moondance Café while she was in town. Becky's mom is great at stuff like that.

Suddenly I heard my name. I thought I must be dreaming.

"Allie?" Becky's mom was standing next to me. "Someone outside would like to meet you. Come with me."

I moved as if I were in a trance. Becky helped me get my apron off.

"I'm pleased to meet you, Allie." Vermilion was looking right into my eyes. "Allison Gray, right? Well, we both seem to have colors for names. And I understand you sing, too?"

"Y-yes." I realized that I'd never *really* been tongue-tied until then. It felt as though my tongue were literally in a knot. I couldn't have spoken if I'd wanted to: Vermilion's bright colors—her hair, her eyes, the emerald green of her silk blouse—overwhelmed me.

"Will I see you in the audience tomorrow night?" she asked.

I couldn't just stand there like a dummy. I had to say something. But just thinking about missing the concert made me feel like crying again. "No," I said, amazed that my voice sounded as steady as it did. "I . . . I t-tried to get a ticket b-but . . . they were sold out."

"Oh, of course," she said. "They told me it was sold out. But wait." She looked across at the older man she was with. "I have two house seats that may be available, right, Dad?" She winked at him and he smiled. So this was Vermilion's *father*!

He smiled at me. "Yes, if my daughter's thinking what I think she's thinking, Allison, you'll be in the audience tomorrow night."

I was stunned but I managed to find my voice.

"Oh, thank you! You have no idea how happy I am! I could . . . I could sing!" And without thinking I leaned over and hugged her.

Vermilion actually hugged me back and said, "I hope you do sing, Allie. I think I have the best job in the world, and I'm sure you'd like it, too. Come backstage after the show and tell me how you liked it. I'll leave your name with the guard—Allison Gray and guest."

"We will!" I said. "Thanks!" I knew just who the "guest" was going to be, too.

Fourteen

You would think I woke Becky at the crack of dawn the next morning, the way she complained.

"Go away," she cried, pulling the covers over her head. "This is my morning to sleep late."

"Oh, Beck, come on. Please, I can't sleep any longer. I have an idea, and I need you to come out and get something with me."

I must have sounded desperate, because Becky pulled the covers off her face for a second and looked at me. "What do you need to get?" she asked.

"Something at the mall."

"It's not open in the middle of the night." Becky rolled over and firmly buried her head under her pillow.

"Becky." I knew if I waited she'd give in. "It's *not* the middle of the night. It's nine-thirty. The mall opens at ten. And I've been waiting for you to get up for an hour already."

"All *right*, all right," Becky moaned. "Just don't rush me."

She got out of bed, dragging her patchwork quilt off the bed behind her. Soon I heard water running.

I checked my watch. We'd probably be ready to leave right around ten. Ever since I'd seen Rosie's fake nails (and had bitten mine to the quick during the biology midterm) I'd wanted to try them. Today was the day. After all, I wanted to look my best for the concert tonight, especially when I went backstage afterward.

"So what is this mysterious something you need to get at the mall?" Becky asked as we bounced down the steps of the Moondance.

"Nails."

"Nails? You need the hardware store, not the mall. What do you need nails for, anyway?"

"No! Not nails, *nails*!" I held out my hands.

"Allie, you're going to wear fake nails?" Becky was curious. "Since when do you care what your nails look like?"

"Since now," I told her. "Becky, I have to look my best tonight. Did you forget we're going to the concert, and backstage afterwards?"

We got to the mall, and I found a drugstore with a pretty big selection of fake nails. They had all sizes and colors. I picked a pale pink set that wasn't too long. I couldn't wait to get home and try them on.

"It will be great to finally have long nails," I said as we walked back to my house.

"Oh, these aren't really long," Becky said. "I've seen some that are so long they look like claws. You know, I read that the Empress of China used to have fingernails two feet long, and all she could do was sit around with her hands on pillows all day."

I looked sideways at Becky. "Fascinating," I said dryly.

When we got back to my house, Becky was really great about helping me get the nails on. And honestly, I don't think I could have gotten them glued on straight if she hadn't been there to help me. Afterward she went home, promising to call me later on so we could figure out what we'd wear to the concert together. Then she'd come over and we'd get dressed at my house.

It was a little peculiar adjusting to long fingernails all of a sudden, but I got the hang of it after a while. Later on, Becky called and we decided to dress up, sort of, in tights and a skirt we each have in a different color. I'd be mostly in shades of purple and Becky would be mostly in red.

When I tried to pull on my plum-colored tights, I realized that even though my nails weren't as long as the Empress of China's there were some things that weren't too easy to do with long nails. As I tried to wiggle my hands down into the tights so I could get them over my legs, my new nails kept getting in the way. They caught on the fabric, and it took me at least ten tries before it finally seemed that I was getting it. In the process, one nail fell off and I had to stop and glue it back on.

I tried again to pull on the tights. I got my hand down without snagging anything and, with a little difficulty, managed to pull one leg up over my knee. Then I pulled the other leg up. The only problem was, I was afraid to really grip the tights firmly, because a nail might pop off (or worse, might poke through the tights). So when I stood up to see how well I'd done, the crotch of my tights was down around my knees, and I didn't know how on earth I could get them any higher.

That's when Becky walked in, her freshly washed hair wrapped in a towel.

"Oh, no! Are you serious?" She laughed until I finally started laughing, too, which was a big mistake because with my tights around my knees my balance was a little shaky. I fell over. Fortunately, my room's not that big, and I landed on the bed.

"Becky, stop laughing," I giggled. "You've got to help me figure out how to get these on."

Becky thought about it for a minute. "Allie, the only thing you can do is take your nails off, *then* put the tights on, and put the nails back on afterward."

I looked at the clock. We had to be ready in forty-five minutes, but Becky was right. It was the only way. I sighed.

With Becky helping, I got the nails off. Finally I was dressed. We had five minutes left. Thirty seconds for each finger! We did it, though, just in the nick of time. As the last one was just setting, I heard my mother call up the stairs, "You girls ready?"

"Yes!" we hollered at the same time as we raced downstairs.

The concert was fantastic. It was like a dream come true. The music was terrific, and our seats were so close to the stage I could almost reach out and touch Vermilion. I was pretty sure she was looking right at me sometimes.

Vermilion wore a silky tunic with matching pants that flowed around her as she sang. The fabric was a deep sapphire blue, and it made her eyes look an even deeper violet-blue.

At the end she came back for an encore. She looked right down where I was sitting and said in that incredible voice of hers, "This is for everyone who has a dream. Follow it, and I'm sure it will come true." Was she talking to me? I wanted to jump up and say, *It has already. I can't believe I'm really here.*

But of course I didn't. Then Vermilion looked past me into the audience and began to sing, "It takes rain to make a rainbow . . . ."

Afterward, Vermilion's dad came on stage and gave her a bouquet of red roses, and the two of them left the stage.

Becky and I made our way backstage. A guard stopped us at the door. "I'm sorry," he said. "You're not allowed back here."

"B-but. . . ." I faltered.

Becky jumped in, "But Vermilion said she'd leave our names with you so we could go back."

The guard seemed a little surprised. "What's your name?"

"I'm Allison Gray," I said. "And this is my friend, Becky Bartlett." He pulled a list from his pocket and looked at it. I kept my fingers crossed. What if Vermilion had forgotten?

The guard looked up at us and smiled. Then he stood aside and held the door open. "Go down this hall and turn right at the end," he told us.

I was glad Becky was with me. As we walked down the long hall, we could hear a murmuring as if lots of people were talking somewhere. It got louder and louder until we turned the corner and found ourselves in the middle of a pretty glamorous party.

There were about forty people there. I recognized

the musicians in Vermilion's band, and I saw some people with cameras who looked like newspaper reporters. There were a lot of older kids who looked like students from the college.

In one corner there was a big table with all sorts of pastries, fruit, cheese, and soft drinks. Even though it was pretty late, I suddenly felt a little hungry. But I was too shy to go up and get something. Becky wasn't, though, and she nudged me up with her.

We had just poured sodas for ourselves when the conversations around us all seemed to stop. I turned around and Vermilion was right next to me. She'd just come in from a door behind me. I could see her dad in back of her.

Vermilion looked right at me and smiled. "Allie, I'm so glad you could make it," she said. "How were the seats?"

"Oh, they were the best," I said. "But you were even better. The concert was fabulous."

"I'm glad you liked it," she said. "So are you going to take my advice?"

I was confused. "I'm not sure I know what you mean," I said.

"Follow your dream, Allie," Vermilion told me. "The other night you told me you sing. What kind of songs do you sing?"

"Well, I mostly like to sing along with your music,

but . . . ." I gulped. "I'm too shy to sing in front of other people, like you do."

"Hmmm. Well, I'm flattered, of course," she said. "But I know what it's like to be shy, believe me. What you have to do is work on developing your own voice and style, and find out what *you* can do. I think you'll find that your shyness will seem less of an obstacle then." She squeezed my hand. "And the more you sing, especially in front of other people, the better you'll feel about it. Promise me you'll try?"

"Yes," I whispered.

"I've heard that you have a great voice." I started to blush, but Vermilion laughed and held up her hand. "No, I'm not going to ask you to sing right here. I just want to tell you that if you have a good voice, it's nothing to be shy about. I only wish I'd learned that earlier in my life," she sighed.

I looked at her in astonishment. "Really?" I squeaked.

"Oh, yes," Vermilion said. "My dad could tell you stories. I was a lot like you, Allie."

I felt as if my eyes were wider than they'd ever been before. Just then a reporter stepped up. "Could I ask you a few questions?"

Vermilion looked at me and winked. "Remember what I said, okay, Allie?"

"I will," I said fervently. "Thank you for everything. This has been the most fabulous night of my whole life!" Suddenly I remembered something. "Would you mind autographing my program before I go?"

"For you, Allie, of course," Vermilion said. She took my program and wrote, in big flourishing letters, "To Allison, from one singer to another. Go for it. Love, Vermilion."

Then she signed Becky's program, too. I was in such a daze after that that it's a good thing Becky was with me. It was pretty late, and my mother was going to be waiting for us outside. I let Becky lead me back down the long hall.

In the car we leaned back against the seats. I was exhausted. I kept going over and over everything Vermilion had said, and remembering the concert and how totally great it had been.

Becky suddenly said, "I can't believe how cool you were when you were talking to Vermilion, Allie. I would have been too nervous even to get a single word out."

"But I *was* nervous, Beck," I said.

"Oh no, you weren't," she said positively.

"How do you know?"

"Because," she sang out triumphantly, "you didn't stammer once!"

I thought about it. Becky was right.

"Hey, Becky," I said. "Will you go with me this week to try out for glee club?"

"Sure," Becky said, "But let's start practicing now, okay?"

We sang "It Takes Rain to Make a Rainbow" all the way home.

Special Party Tip
Allie's "Prehistoric Ice Cream"

You don't have to wait until you're stuck with the wrong birthday cake to make this treat, and children—and grown-ups—love it!

Shopping List: Several quarts of ice cream in different favorite flavors, such as chocolate, banana, mint chip, cherry swirl. (Use your imagination and take your party guests' preferences into account.)

1 bag of candy. (Allie used gummy dinosaurs, but you can use jellybeans or miniature candy bars, too.)

1 box of crunchy cookies, such as graham crackers, chocolate chips or cream sandwiches.

Then get out as many bowls as you need. Place a candy treat in the bottom of each bowl (but make sure it's unwrapped!). Then spoon in a scoop of every flavor ice cream. Stick the cookie in the top and you're ready to serve Allie's Prehistoric Ice Cream. Note: You can also put a candy treat in only one bowl and give a prize to the person who gets that serving.

What Has the Party Line Gotten Into?

"Aaagh!" everyone cried at once. Pillows flew at me from all directions, but I hardly felt them. I was still in a state of shock. We had been hired to throw a birthday party for one of our *classmates*—and not just any classmate, either. Cascy Wyatt was the most obnoxious boy ever to pass through the halls of Canfield Middle School.

Special bonus chapter from
***The Party Line #2,* Julie's Boy Problem:**
turn page.

One

"Hey, Rosie," I whispered to my best friend. "Doesn't Mark Harris look good today?"

She turned and rolled her eyes at me. "Yes, he does. Just like yesterday and the day before and the day before that. Now will you please shut up and pay attention?"

I shrugged. I couldn't help it. All I had been thinking about lately was how incredibly cute Mark was. Even though we were sitting in biology class and I was supposed to be taking notes, I kept sneaking looks across the room at Mark. I was trying to be cool about it, because I'd die if he ever suspected I liked him *that* way. Mark and I have kind of been buddies for a year or so, ever since we discovered we were both major Red Sox fans. When we talk, it's always been about games and stats and stuff like that. I don't know how I never managed to notice before how adorable he is.

But lately I haven't been able *not* to notice. He's like a younger version of River Phoenix. I mean, he's *that* cute.

Rosie nudged me and passed me a note. It read, "Hey, Berger, listen up!" and was signed "Becky and Allie." Becky Bartlett and Allison Gray are my two other best friends, besides Rosie. We're all in the seventh grade together, and biology is our absolute *least* favorite class.

They sit right behind me and Rosie, so I turned around and stuck out my tongue at them.

"Julie, is there something in the back of the room that the rest of us should know about?" Ms. Pernell asked.

I swiveled my head back toward the front of the room. "Uh, no," I said guiltily. "I thought I heard something." As I spoke, I could feel the most intense blush spreading across my face. I was so embarrassed—I knew Mark would be looking at me, because everyone in the class was. Although I'm a pretty good student, I get in trouble a lot because it's hard to be in class with your three best friends in the world and not talk all period!

"Well, why don't you just watch what I'm going to write on the board now," Ms. Pernell said in a slightly angry voice. She picked up her chalk and wrote our homework assignment on the blackboard.

"On Monday, we're going to begin our frog dissections," she announced, and a couple of kids in the class groaned. "It's nothing to worry about," Ms. Pernell went on. "We'll be working in pairs, the way all great researchers do." She chuckled as if she had just made the funniest joke in the world. Then she went to her desk and picked up her clipboard. "Now, let's see . . . Rick Addison, you will be working with Rosie Torres. Becky Bartlett, you'll be with . . ."

"I can't believe Mark Harris is my lab partner!" I cried. "This is the worst! I just know I'll freak when I have to touch that stupid frog!"

"Or when Mark sits next to you," Rosie joked. We were walking along the sidewalk on our way home after school. Usually we take the bus, but I made her walk with me that day because I couldn't talk about Mark with anyone else around. And I just *had* to talk about him.

"I just hope I don't do something incredibly dumb," I said.

"You won't," Rosie assured me, shifting her backpack from one shoulder to the other. "You're good at that kind of stuff. Remember how you used to do surgery on my dolls when their arms got broken?"

"Yeah." I smiled. "But they weren't all green and slimy. And they didn't have real guts and junk like that."

"Julie! Yuck!" Rosie wrinkled her nose in disgust.

"Rosie, don't make a face like that!"

"Why not? If you can say something so unbelievably gross, why can't I make a face?"

"Because," I said, "your face might freeze like that."

"Ha, ha." Rosie didn't think my joke was very funny.

"Sorry, just kidding. But really, you shouldn't do it because it can give you wrinkles."

"Get out, Julie. I never heard anything so dumb."

"It's true. Heather told me. She read it in some fashion magazine." Heather is my oldest sister, and if anyone is a beauty expert, she is. She's eighteen— and totally gorgeous.

"Really, though, what am I going to do?" I asked Rosie. "I just know I'll do something stupid in bio."

"I think we should be more worried about what *Becky* is going to do. She can't even open her locker without help. Giving her a knife and a dead frog is really asking for trouble."

Rosie was right. Our friend Becky is so clumsy that her parents won't let her near any of the breakable stuff, like china and glassware, in the restaurant they own, the Moondance Café. It's as if there is some kind of jinx around her. At least I'm fairly coordinated. You really have to be if you're athletic, like I am. I'm pretty good at sports, especially baseball. Rosie's pretty coordinated, too. She has to be to polish her nails as perfectly as she does!

When we turned the corner, a group of about six

boys from our class went riding past us on their bikes. Casey Wyatt, the most obnoxious boy in our class, was out in front making siren noises. Mark was in the group, too. "Oh no," I hissed to Rosie. "What if he heard me? I'll die!"

Rosie shook her head. "No way. He couldn't have."

Just then Casey made a sharp turn away from the group and nearly ran me over. What a creep!

"Hey, Berger!" he yelled. "Nice going in bio today!"

Rosie and I ignored him.

"What were you looking for in the back of the room, anyway?" Casey asked loudly. "A boyfriend?"

"No, I was looking for your brain," I said. "But I didn't see it anywhere."

Rosie burst out laughing. The other guys were waiting up for Casey and they laughed, too—even Mark. I couldn't help smiling, even though Casey looked really mad.

"Hey, you're blinding me, tinsel teeth!" Casey yelled.

I shut my mouth immediately. I *hate* having braces. Leave it to that rotten Casey Wyatt to say the worst possible thing in the world. In front of Mark, too! I felt a horrible blush creeping over my face for the second time that day. I hoped Mark couldn't see it. He was circling around on his bike behind Casey, so I don't think he was looking at me.

Rosie and I just kept walking, and I looked straight ahead.

"Let's get out of here," I heard Casey say. "We have better things to do than stand around talking to girls." With that, he turned his bike around and sped off down the street. The others followed. I had never thought I'd be glad to see Mark Harris disappear from sight, but that time I was.

"Casey Wyatt is such a—such a dweeb!" I shouted once they were out of earshot. "He makes me so mad!" I'd never give him the satisfaction of knowing how much his teasing upsets me. That wasn't the first time he'd said something mean, but it was definitely the worst. I felt awful.

"Just ignore him," said Rosie.

"Why do those other guys hang out with him?" I asked.

"I guess they think he's funny." Rosie shrugged. "He just hates girls."

"Well, I hate *him*," I said. I know that probably sounds a little extreme, but that's how I felt.

"Listen, I'll call you tomorrow," Rosie said when we reached my street. "And don't worry about the lab on Monday, okay?"

"Yeah, right. My braces are blinding, I don't want to touch a dead frog, and my lab partner is Mark Harris. What do I have to worry about?" I couldn't help being a little sarcastic. But Rosie was my friend and she was trying to cheer me up. "Okay, I won't worry. Thanks for listening, Rosie. See you later."

As soon as I walked in the door, my mother called out, "Julie? Is that you?" I swear, my mom can see through walls. No matter who comes in, she always knows who it is, even if she happens to be in another part of the house at the time.

"Yes, Mom, it's me." I dropped my books on the bottom step of the stairway and wandered toward the kitchen. It was a mistake, though, because I had to pass through the dining room, which has a big mirror on one wall. I stopped in front of it and smiled at my reflection. My looks had never bothered me before, but now I felt like a big brace face. How could I ever expect Mark to fall in love with a metal mouth like me? Not that I really wanted him to fall in *love*, exactly. I just wouldn't mind if he fell in *like*. Couldn't they invent braces that you only had to wear for two weeks instead of two years?

Why couldn't I be beautiful like my older sisters? Maybe I'm going to improve with age, but that wasn't going to do me any good right then. The more I looked at myself, the worse I felt. It wasn't that I thought I was ugly. I just felt pitifully average. I have straight honey-blond hair and blue eyes, and I'm kind of on the skinny side. *Maybe I should give up sports,* I thought to myself. *Maybe then I'll look more like how a girl is supposed to look.*

"I can't believe it, Julie," my mother called from

the kitchen. "You've been in the house for at least five minutes and you haven't started eating yet."

I went in and rummaged through the refrigerator, but I just didn't feel like eating anything. My cat, Dizzy, was in the kitchen, too, trying to get some milk for herself. She rubbed up against my legs and purred loudly.

"See anything that looks good?" my mom asked.

"Uh-uh," I said, squatting down to pick up Dizzy.

"What's wrong?" my mother asked. "Why do you look so tragic? Smile a little."

"I'm never going to smile again," I said dramatically. "I wouldn't want to blind anyone."

Mom motioned toward the table. "Sit down," she said. I plunked down on a chair, with Dizzy on my lap. "Don't you remember when Heather had braces?"

"No, not really," I said. "Did she wear them in her sleep or something?"

"No, silly. She had them when she was your age. But you probably don't remember them because you got so used to seeing them," my mother explained.

"Mom, do you expect me to believe that nobody notices I have braces?" I asked her.

"No, honey. It's just that they're not such a big deal," she said.

Not a big deal? I said to myself. Sometimes my mother doesn't know what she's talking about. "Mom, I'm going upstairs for a while," I said, standing up. I carried Dizzy upstairs to the bathroom and looked at my metallic smile in the mirror again.

"When you're trying to get Mark Harris to like you, braces are a very big deal," I told my cat. "You're just lucky you don't have any." Then I made a very important decision. From that moment on, I would open my mouth as little as possible in public.

I wouldn't even eat.